# EVE'S RANSOM

## George Gissing

Dover Publications, Inc.
New York

Published in Canada by General Publishing Company, Ltd.,
30 Lesmill Road, Don Mills, Toronto, Ontario.
Published in the United Kingdom by Constable and Company, Ltd., 10 Orange Street, London WC2H 7EG.

This Dover edition, first published in 1980, is an unabridged and unaltered republication of the work originally published by Lawrence & Bullen in 1895.

International Standard Book Number: 0-486-24016-9
Library of Congress Catalog Card Number: 80-67317

Manufactured in the United States of America
Dover Publications, Inc.
180 Varick Street
New York, N.Y. 10014

# CHAPTER I

On the station platform at Dudley Port, in the dusk of a February afternoon, half-a-dozen people waited for the train to Birmingham. A south-west wind had loaded the air with moisture, which dripped at moments, thinly and sluggishly, from a featureless sky. The lamps, just lighted, cast upon wet wood and metal a pale yellow shimmer; voices sounded with peculiar clearness; so did the rumble of a porter's barrow laden with luggage. From a foundry hard by came the muffled, rhythmic thunder of mighty blows; this and the long note of an engine-whistle wailing far off seemed to intensify the stillness of the air as gloomy day passed into gloomier night.

In clear daylight the high, uncovered platform would have offered an outlook over the surrounding country, but at this hour no horizon was discernible. Buildings near at hand, rude masses of grimy brick, stood out against a grey confused background; among them rose a turret which vomited crimson flame. This fierce, infernal glare seemed to lack the irradiating quality of earthly fires; with hard, though fluctuating outline, it leapt towards the kindred night, and diffused a blotchy darkness. In the opposite direction, over towards Dudley Town, appeared spots of lurid glow. But on the scarred and barren plain which extends to Birmingham there had settled so thick an obscurity, vapours from above blending with earthly reek, that all the beacons of fiery toil were wrapped and hidden.

Of the waiting travellers, two kept apart from the rest, pacing this way and that, but independently of each other. They were men of dissimilar appearance; the one comfortably and expensively dressed, his age about fifty, his visage bearing the stamp of commerce; the other, younger by more than twenty years, habited in a way which made it difficult to ascertain his social standing, and looking about him with eyes suggestive of anything but prudence or content. Now and then they exchanged a glance: he of the high hat and caped ulster betrayed an interest in the younger man, who, in his turn, took occasion to observe the other from a distance, with show of dubious recognition.

1

The trill of an electric signal, followed by a clanging bell, brought them both to a pause, and they stood only two or three yards apart. Presently a light flashed through the thickening dusk; there was roaring, grinding, creaking and a final yell of brake-tortured wheels. Making at once for the nearest third-class carriage, the man in the seedy overcoat sprang to a place, and threw himself carelessly back; a moment, and he was followed by the second passenger, who seated himself on the opposite side of the compartment. Once more they looked at each other, but without change of countenance.

Tickets were collected, for there would be no stoppage before Birmingham: then the door slammed, and the two men were alone together.

Two or three minutes after the train had started, the elder man leaned forward, moved slightly, and spoke.

"Excuse me, I think your name must be Hilliard."

"What then?" was the brusque reply.

"You don't remember me?"

"Scoundrels are common enough," returned the other, crossing his legs, "but I remember you for all that."

The insult was thrown out with a peculiarly reckless air; it astounded the hearer, who sat for an instant with staring eyes and lips apart; then the blood rushed to his cheeks.

"If I hadn't just about twice your muscle, my lad," he answered angrily, "I'd make you repent that, and be more careful with your tongue in future. Now, mind what you say! We've a quiet quarter of an hour before us, and I might alter my mind."

The young man laughed contemptuously. He was tall, but slightly built, and had delicate hands.

"So you've turned out a blackguard, have you?" pursued his companion, whose name was Dengate. "I heard something about that."

"From whom?"

"You drink, I am told. I suppose that's your condition now."

"Well, no; not just now," answered Hilliard. He spoke the language of an educated man, but with a trace of the Midland accent. Dengate's speech had less refinement.

"What do you mean by your insulting talk, then? I spoke to you civilly."

"And I answered as I thought fit."

The respectable citizen sat with his hands on his knees, and scrutinised the other's sallow features.

"You've been drinking, I can see. I had something to say to you, but I'd better leave it for another time."

Hilliard flashed a look of scorn, and said sternly—

"I am as sober as you are."

"Then just give me civil answers to civil questions."

"Questions? What right have you to question me?"

"It's for your own advantage. You called me scoundrel. What did you mean by that?"

"That's the name I give to fellows who go bankrupt to get rid of their debts."

"Is it!" said Dengate, with a superior smile. "That only shows how little you know of the world, my lad. You got it from your father, I daresay; he had a rough way of talking."

"A disagreeable habit of telling the truth."

"I know all about it. Your father wasn't a man of business, and couldn't see things from a business point of view. Now, what I just want to say to you is this: there's all the difference in the world between commercial failure and rascality. If you go down to Liverpool, and ask men of credit for their opinion about Charles Edward Dengate, you'll have a lesson that would profit you. I can see you're one of the young chaps who think a precious deal of themselves; I'm often coming across them nowadays, and I generally give them a piece of my mind."

Hilliard smiled.

"If you gave them the whole, it would be no great generosity."

"Eh? Yes, I see you've had a glass or two, and it makes you witty. But wait a bit. I was devilish near thrashing you a few minutes ago; but I shan't do it, say what you like. I don't like vulgar rows."

"No more do I," remarked Hilliard; "and I haven't fought since I was a boy. But for your own satisfaction, I can tell you it's a wise resolve not to interfere with me. The temptation to rid the world of one such man as you might prove too strong."

There was a force of meaning in these words, quietly as they were uttered, which impressed the listener.

"You'll come to a bad end, my lad."

"Hardly. It's unlikely that I shall ever be rich."

"Oh! you're one of that sort, are you? I've come across Socialistic fellows. But look here. I'm talking civilly, and I say again it's for your advantage. I had a respect for your father, and I liked your brother— I'm sorry to hear he's dead."

"Please keep your sorrow to yourself."

"All right, all right! I understand you're a draughtsman at Kenn and Bodditch's?"

"I daresay you are capable of understanding that."

Hilliard planted his elbow in the window of the carriage and propped his cheek on his hand.

"Yes; and a few other things," rejoined the well-dressed man. "How to make money, for instance.—Well, haven't you any insult ready?"

The other looked out at a row of flaring chimneys, which the train was rushing past: he kept silence.

"Go down to Liverpool," pursued Dengate, "and make inquiries about me. You'll find I have as good a reputation as any man living."

He laboured this point. It was evident that he seriously desired to establish his probity and importance in the young man's eyes. Nor did anything in his look or speech conflict with such claims. He had hard, but not disagreeable features, and gave proof of an easy temper.

"Paying one's debts," said Hilliard, "is fatal to reputation."

"You use words you don't understand. There's no such thing as a debt, except what's recognised by the laws."

"I shouldn't wonder if you think of going into Parliament. You are just the man to make laws."

"Well, who knows? What I want you to understand is, that if your father were alive at this moment, I shouldn't admit that he had claim upon me for one penny."

"It was because I understood it already that I called you a scoundrel."

"Now be careful, my lad," exclaimed Dengate, as again he winced under the epithet. "My temper may get the better of me, and I should be sorry for it. I got into this carriage with you (of course I had a first-class ticket) because I wanted to form an opinion of your character. I've been told you drink, and I see that you do, and I'm sorry for it. You'll be losing your place before long, and you'll go down. Now look here; you've called me foul names, and you've done your best to rile me. Now I'm going to make you ashamed of yourself."

Hilliard fixed the speaker with his scornful eyes; the last words had moved him to curiosity.

"I can excuse a good deal in a man with an empty pocket," pursued the other. "I've been there myself; I know how it makes you feel— how much do you earn, by the bye?"

"Mind your own business."

"All right. I suppose it's about two pounds a week. Would you like to know what *my* income is? Well, something like two pounds an hour, reckoning eight hours as the working day. There's a difference, isn't there? It comes of minding my business, you see. You'll never make anything like it; you find it easier to abuse people who work than to work yourself. Now if you go down to Liverpool, and ask how I got to my present position, you'll find it's the result of hard and honest work. Understand that: honest work."

"And forgetting to pay your debts," threw in the young man.

"It's eight years since I owed any man a penny. The people I *did* owe money to were sensible men of business—all except your father, and he never could see things in the right light. I went through the bankruptcy court, and I made arrangements that satisfied my creditors. I should have satisfied your father too, only he died."

"You paid tuppence ha'penny in the pound."

"No, it was five shillings, and my creditors—sensible men of business—were satisfied. Now look here. I owed your father four hundred and thirty-six pounds, but he didn't rank as an ordinary creditor, and if I had paid him after my bankruptcy it would have been just because I felt a respect for him—not because he had any legal claim. I *meant* to pay him—understand that."

Hilliard smiled. Just then a block signal caused the train to slacken speed. Darkness had fallen, and lights glimmered from some cottages by the line.

"You don't believe me," added Dengate.

"I don't."

The prosperous man bit his lower lip, and sat gazing at the lamp in the carriage. The train came to a standstill; there was no sound but the throbbing of the engine.

"Well, listen to me," Dengate resumed. "You're turning out badly, and any money you get you're pretty sure to make a bad use of. But"— he assumed an air of great solemnity—"all the same—now listen——"

"I'm listening."

"Just to show you the kind of a man I am, and to make you feel ashamed of yourself, I'm going to pay you the money."

For a few seconds there was unbroken stillness. The men gazed at each other, Dengate superbly triumphant, Hilliard incredulous but betraying excitement.

"I'm going to pay you four hundred and thirty-six pounds," Dengate repeated. "No less and no more. It isn't a legal debt, so I shall pay no interest. But go with me when we get to Birmingham, and you shall have my cheque for four hundred and thirty-six pounds."

The train began to move on. Hilliard had uncrossed his legs, and sat bending forward, his eyes on vacancy.

"Does that alter your opinion of me?" asked the other.

"I shan't believe it till I have cashed the cheque."

"You're one of those young fellows who think so much of themselves they've no good opinion to spare for anyone else. And what's more, I've still half a mind to give you a good thrashing before I give you the cheque. There's just about time, and I shouldn't wonder if it did you good. You want some of the conceit taken out of you, my lad."

Hilliard seemed not to hear this. Again he fixed his eyes on the other's countenance.

"Do you say you are going to pay me four hundred pounds?" he asked slowly.

"Four hundred and thirty-six. You'll go to the devil with it, but that's no business of mine."

"There's just one thing I must tell you. If this is a joke, keep out of my way after you've played it out, that's all."

"It isn't a joke. And one thing I have to tell *you*. I reserve to myself the right of thrashing you, if I feel in the humour for it."

Hilliard gave a laugh, then threw himself back into the corner, and did not speak again until the train pulled up at New Street station.

## CHAPTER II

An hour later he was at Old Square, waiting for the tram to Aston. Huge steam-driven vehicles came and went, whirling about the open space with monitory bell-clang. Amid a press of homeward-going workfolk, Hilliard clambered to a place on the top and lit his pipe. He did not look the same man who had waited gloomily at Dudley Port; his eyes gleamed with life; answering a remark addressed to him by a neighbour on the car, he spoke jovially.

No rain was falling, but the streets shone wet and muddy under lurid lamp-lights. Just above the house-tops appeared the full moon, a reddish disk, blurred athwart floating vapour. The car drove northward, speedily passing from the region of main streets and great edifices into a squalid district of factories and workshops and crowded by-ways. At Aston Church the young man alighted, and walked rapidly for five minutes, till he reached a row of small modern houses. Socially, they represented a step or two upwards in the gradation which, at Birmingham, begins with the numbered court and culminates in the mansions of Edgbaston.

He knocked at a door, and was answered by a girl, who nodded recognition.

"Mrs. Hilliard in? Just tell her I'm here."

There was a natural abruptness in his voice, but it had a kindly note, and a pleasant smile accompanied it. After a brief delay he received permission to go upstairs, where the door of a sitting-room stood open. Within was a young woman, slight, pale, and pretty, who showed something of embarrassment, though her face made him welcome.

"I expected you sooner."

"Business kept me back. Well, little girl?"

The table was spread for tea, and at one end of it, on a high chair, sat a child of four years old. Hilliard kissed her, and stroked her curly hair, and talked with playful affection. This little girl was his niece, the child of his elder brother, who had died three years ago. The poorly furnished room and her own attire proved that Mrs. Hilliard had but narrow resources in her widowhood. Nor did she appear a woman of much courage; tears had thinned her cheeks, and her delicate hands had suffered noticeably from unwonted household work.

Hilliard remarked something unusual in her behaviour this evening. She was restless, and kept regarding him askance, as if in apprehension. A letter from her, in which she merely said she wished to speak to him, had summoned him hither from Dudley. As a rule, they saw each other but once a month.

"No bad news, I hope!" he remarked aside to her, as he took his place at the table.

"Oh, no. I'll tell you afterwards."

Very soon after the meal Mrs. Hilliard took the child away and put her to bed. During her absence the visitor sat brooding, a peculiar half-smile on his face. She came back, drew a chair up to the fire, but did not sit down.

"Well, what is it?" asked her brother-in-law, much as he might have spoken to the little girl.

"I have something very serious to talk about, Maurice."

"Have you? All right; go ahead."

"I—I am so very much afraid I shall offend you."

The young man laughed.

"Not very likely. I can take a good deal from you."

She stood with her hands on the back of the chair, and as he looked at her, Hilliard saw her pale cheeks grow warm.

"It'll seem very strange to you, Maurice."

"Nothing will seem strange after an adventure I've had this afternoon. You shall hear about it presently."

"Tell me your story first."

"That's like a woman. All right, I'll tell you. I met that scoundrel Dengate, and—he's paid me the money he owed my father."

"He has *paid* it? Oh! really?"

"See, here's a cheque, and I think it likely I can turn it into cash. The blackguard has been doing well at Liverpool. I'm not quite sure that I understand the reptile, but he seems to have given me this because I abused him. I hurt his vanity, and he couldn't resist the temptation to astonish me. He thinks I shall go about proclaiming him a noble fellow. Four hundred and thirty-six pounds; there it is."

He tossed the piece of paper into the air with boyish glee, and only just caught it as it was fluttering into the fire.

"Oh, be careful!" cried Mrs. Hilliard.

"I told him he was a scoundrel, and he began by threatening to thrash me. I'm very glad he didn't try. It was in the train, and I know very well I should have strangled him. It would have been awkward, you know."

"Oh, Maurice, how *can* you——?"

"Well, here's the money; and half of it is yours."

"Mine? Oh, no! After all you have given me. Besides, I sha'n't want it."

"How's that?"

Their eyes met. Hilliard again saw the flush in her cheeks, and began to guess its explanation. He looked puzzled, interested.

"Do I know him?" was his next inquiry.

"Should you think it very wrong of me?" She moved aside from the line of his gaze. "I couldn't imagine how you would take it."

"It all depends. Who is the man?"

Still shrinking towards a position where Hilliard could not easily observe her, the young widow told her story. She had consented to marry a man of whom her brother-in-law knew little but the name, one Ezra Marr; he was turned forty, a widower without children, and belonged to a class of small employers of labour known in Birmingham as "little masters." The contrast between such a man and Maurice Hilliard's brother was sufficiently pronounced; but the widow nervously did her best to show Ezra Marr in a favourable light.

"And then," she added after a pause, while Hilliard was reflecting, "I couldn't go on being a burden on you. How very few men would have done what you have——"

"Stop a minute. Is *that* the real reason? If so——"

Hurriedly she interposed.

"That was only one of the reasons—only one."

Hilliard knew very well that her marriage had not been entirely successful; it seemed to him very probable that with a husband of the artisan class, a vigorous and go-ahead fellow, she would be better mated than in the former instance. He felt sorry for his little niece, but there again sentiment doubtless conflicted with common-sense. A few more questions, and it became clear to him that he had no ground of resistance.

"Very well. Most likely you are doing a wise thing. And half this money is yours; you'll find it useful."

The discussion of this point was interrupted by a tap at the door. Mrs. Hilliard, after leaving the room for a moment, returned with rosy countenance.

"He is here," she murmured. "I thought I should like you to meet him this evening. Do you mind?"

Mr. Marr entered; a favourable specimen of his kind; strong, comely, frank of look and speech. Hilliard marvelled somewhat at his choice of the frail and timid little widow, and hoped upon marriage would follow no repentance. A friendly conversation between the two men confirmed them in mutual good opinion. At length Mrs. Hilliard spoke of the offer of money made by her brother-in-law.

"I don't feel I've any right to it," she said, after explaining the circumstances. "You know what Maurice has done for me. I've always felt I was robbing him——"

"I wanted to say something about that," put in the bass-voiced Ezra. "I want to tell you, Mr. Hilliard, that you're a man I'm proud to know, and proud to shake hands with. And if my view goes for anything, Emily won't take a penny of what you're offering her. I should think it wrong and mean. It is about time—that's my way of thinking—that you looked after your own interests. Emily has no claim to a share in this money, and what's more, I don't wish her to take it."

"Very well," said Hilliard. "I tell you what we'll do. A couple of hundred pounds shall be put aside for the little girl. You can't make any objection to that."

The mother glanced doubtfully at her future husband, but Marr again spoke with emphasis.

"Yes, I do object. If you don't mind me saying it, I'm quite able to look after the little girl; and the fact is, I want her to grow up looking to me as her father, and getting all she has from me only. Of course, I mean nothing but what's friendly: but there it is; I'd rather Winnie didn't have the money."

This man was in the habit of speaking his mind; Hilliard understood that any insistence would only disturb the harmony of the occasion. He waved a hand, smiled good-naturedly, and said no more.

About nine o'clock he left the house and walked to Aston Church. While he stood there, waiting for the tram, a voice fell upon his ear that caused him to look round. Crouched by the entrance to the churchyard was a beggar in filthy rags, his face hideously bandaged, before him on the pavement a little heap of matchboxes; this creature kept uttering a meaningless sing-song, either idiot jabber, or calculated to excite attention and pity; it sounded something like "A-pah-pahky; pah-pahky; pah"; repeated a score of times, and resumed after a pause. Hilliard gazed and listened, then placed a copper in the wretch's extended palm, and turned away muttering, "What a cursed world!"

He was again on the tram-car before he observed that the full moon, risen into a sky now clear of grosser vapours, gleamed brilliant silver above the mean lights of earth. And round about it, in so vast a circumference that it was only detected by the wandering eye, spread a softly radiant halo. This vision did not long occupy his thoughts, but at intervals he again looked upward, to dream for a moment on the silvery splendour and on that wide halo dim-glimmering athwart the track of stars.


## CHAPTER III

Instead of making for the railway station, to take a train back to Dudley, he crossed from the northern to the southern extremity of the town, and by ten o'clock was in one of the streets which lead out of Moseley Road. Here, at a house such as lodges young men in business, he made inquiry for "Mr. Narramore," and was forthwith admitted.

Robert Narramore, a long-stemmed pipe at his lips, sat by the fireside; on the table lay the materials of a satisfactory supper—a cold fowl, a ham, a Stilton cheese, and a bottle of wine.

"Hollo! You?" he exclaimed, without rising. "I was going to write to you; thanks for saving me the trouble. Have something to eat?"

"Yes, and to drink likewise."

"Do you mind ringing the bell? I believe there's a bottle of Burgundy left. If not, plenty of Bass."

He stretched forth a languid hand, smiling amiably. Narramore was the image of luxurious indolence; he had pleasant features, dark hair inclined to curliness, a well-built frame set off by good tailoring. His income from the commercial house in which he held a post of responsibility would have permitted him to occupy better quarters than these; but here he had lived for ten years, and he preferred a few inconveniences to the trouble of moving. Trouble of any kind was Robert's bugbear. His progress up the commercial ladder seemed due rather to the luck which favours amiable and good-looking young fellows than to any special ability or effort of his own. The very sound of his voice had a drowsiness which soothed—if it did not irritate—the listener.

"Tell them to lay out the truckle-bed," said Hilliard, when he had pulled the bell. "I shall stay here to-night."

"Good!"

Their talk was merely interjectional, until the visitor had begun to appease his hunger and had drawn the cork of a second bottle of bitter ale.

"This is a great day," Hilliard then exclaimed. "I left Dudley this afternoon feeling ready to cut my throat. Now I'm a free man, with the world before me."

"How's that?"

"Emily's going to take a second husband—that's one thing."

"Heaven be praised! Better than one could have looked for."

Hilliard related the circumstances. Then he drew from his pocket an oblong slip of paper, and held it out.

"Dengate?" cried his friend. "How the deuce did you get hold of this?"

Explanation followed. They debated Dengate's character and motives.

"I can understand it," said Narramore. "When I was a boy of twelve I once cheated an apple-woman out of three-halfpence. At the age of sixteen I encountered the old woman again, and felt immense satisfaction in giving her a shilling. But then, you see, I had done with petty cheating; I wished to clear my conscience, and look my fellow-woman in the face."

"That's it, no doubt. He seems to have got some sort of position in Liverpool society, and he didn't like the thought that there was a poor devil at Dudley who went about calling him a scoundrel. By-the-bye, someone told him that I had taken to liquor, and was on my way to destruction generally. I don't know who it could be."

"Oh, we all have candid friends that talk about us."

"It's true I have been drunk now and then of late. There's much to be said for getting drunk."

"Much," assented Narramore, philosophically.

Hilliard went on with his supper; his friend puffed tobacco, and idly regarded the cheque he was still holding.

"And what are you going to do?" he asked at length.

There came no reply, and several minutes passed in silence. Then Hilliard rose from the table, paced the floor once or twice, selected a cigar from a box that caught his eye, and, in cutting off the end, observed quietly——

"I'm going to live."

"Wait a minute. We'll have the table cleared, and a kettle on the fire."

While the servant was busy, Hilliard stood with an elbow on the mantelpiece, thoughtfully smoking his cigar. At Narramore's request, he mixed two tumblers of whisky toddy, then took a draught from his own, and returned to his former position.

"Can't you sit down?" said Narramore.

"No, I can't."

"What a fellow you are! With nerves like yours, I should have been in my grave years ago. You're going to live, eh?"

"Going to be a machine no longer. Can I call myself a man? There's precious little difference between a fellow like me and the damned grinding mechanism that I spend my days in drawing—that roars all day in my ears and deafens me. I'll put an end to that. Here's four hundred pounds. It shall mean four hundred pounds'-worth of life. While this money lasts, I'll feel that I'm a human being."

"Something to be said for that," commented the listener, in his tone of drowsy impartiality.

"I offered Emily half of it. She didn't want to take it, and the man Marr wouldn't let her. I offered to lay it aside for the child, but Marr wouldn't have that either. It's fairly mine."

"Undoubtedly."

"Think! The first time in my life that I've had money on which no one else had a claim. When the poor old father died, Will and I had to go shares in keeping up the home. Our sister couldn't earn anything; she had her work set in attending to her mother. When mother died, and Marian married, it looked as if I had only myself to look after: then came Will's death, and half my income went to keep his wife and child from the workhouse. You know very well I've never grudged it. It's my faith that we do what we do because anything else would be less agreeable. It was more to my liking to live on a pound a week than to see Emily and the little lass suffer want. I've no right to any thanks or praise for it. But the change has come none too soon. There'd have been a paragraph in the Dudley paper some rainy morning."

"Yes, I was rather afraid of that," said Narramore musingly.

He let a minute elapse, whilst his friend paced the room; then added in the same voice:

"We're in luck at the same time. My uncle Sol was found dead this morning."

"Do you come in for much?"

"We don't know what he's left, but I'm down for a substantial fraction in a will he made three years ago. Nobody knew it, but he's been stark mad for the last six months. He took a bed-room out Bordesley way, in a false name, and stored it with a ton or two of tinned meats and vegetables. There the landlady found him lying dead this morning; she learnt who he was from the papers in his pocket. It's come out that he had made friends with some old boozer of that neighbourhood; he told him that England was on the point of a grand financial smash, and that half the population would die of hunger. To secure himself, he began to lay in the stock of tinned provisions. One can't help laughing, poor old chap! That's the result, you see, of a life spent in sweating for money. As a young man he had hard times, and when his invention succeeded, it put him off balance a bit. I've often thought he had a crazy look in his eye. He may have thrown away a lot of his money in mad tricks: who knows?"

"That's the end the human race will come to," said Hilliard. "It'll be driven mad and killed off by machinery. Before long there'll be machines for washing and dressing people—machines for feeding them—machines for——"

His wrathful imagination led him to grotesque ideas which ended in laughter.

"Well, I have a year or two before me. I'll know what enjoyment means. And afterwards——"

"Yes; what afterwards?"

"I don't know. I may choose to come back; I may prefer to make an end. Impossible to foresee my state of mind after living humanly for a year or two. And what shall *you* do if you come in for a lot of money?"

"It's not likely to be more than a few thousands," replied Narramore. "And the chances are I shall go on in the old way. What's the good of a few thousands? I haven't the energy to go off and enjoy myself in your fashion. One of these days I may think of getting married, and marriage, you know, is devilish expensive. I should like to have three or four thousand a year; you can't start housekeeping on less, if you're not to be bored to death with worries. Perhaps I may get a partnership in our house. I began life in the brass bedstead line, and I may as well stick to brass bedsteads to the end: the demand isn't likely to fall off. Please fill my glass again."

Hilliard, the while, had tossed off his second tumbler. He began to talk at random.

"I shall go to London first of all. I may go abroad. Reckon a pound a day. Three hundred and—how many days are there in a year? Three hundred and sixty-five. That doesn't allow me two years. I want two years of life. Half a sovereign a day, then. One can do a good deal with half a sovereign a day—don't you think?"

"Not very much, if you're particular about your wine."

"Wine doesn't matter. Honest ale and Scotch whisky will serve well enough. Understand me; I'm not going in for debauchery, and I'm not going to play the third-rate swell. There's no enjoyment in making a beast of oneself, and none for me in strutting about the streets like an animated figure out of a tailor's window. I want to know the taste of free life, human life. I want to forget that I ever sat at a desk, drawing to scale—drawing damned machines. I want to——"

He checked himself. Narramore looked at him with curiosity.

"It's a queer thing to me, Hilliard," he remarked, when his friend turned away, "that you've kept so clear of women. Now, anyone would think you were just the fellow to get hobbled in that way."

"I daresay," muttered the other. "Yes, it *is* a queer thing. I have been saved, I suppose, by the necessity of supporting my relatives. I've seen so much of women suffering from poverty that it has got me into the habit of thinking of them as nothing but burdens to a man."

"As they nearly always are."

"Yes, nearly always."

Narramore pondered with his amiable smile; the other, after a moment's gloom, shook himself free again, and talked with growing exhilaration of the new life that had dawned before him.

## CHAPTER IV

Hilliard's lodgings—they were represented by a single room—commanded a prospect which, to him a weariness and a disgust, would have seemed impressive enough to eyes beholding it for the first time. On the afternoon of his last day at Dudley he stood by the window and looked forth, congratulating himself, with a fierceness of emotion which defied misgiving, that he would gaze no more on this scene of his servitude.

The house was one of a row situated on a terrace, above a muddy declivity marked with footpaths. It looked over a wide expanse of waste ground, covered in places with coarse herbage, but for the most part undulating in bare tracts of slag and cinder. Opposite, some quarter of a mile away, rose a lofty dome-shaped hill, tree-clad from base to summit, and rearing above the bare branches of its topmost trees the ruined keep of Dudley Castle. Along the foot of this hill ran the highway which descends from Dudley town—hidden by rising ground on the left—to the low-lying railway-station; there, beyond, the eye traversed a great plain, its limit the blending of earth and sky in lurid cloud. A ray of yellow sunset touched the height and its crowning ruin; at the zenith shone a space of pure pale blue: save for these points of relief the picture was colourless and uniformly sombre. Far and near, innumerable chimneys sent forth fumes of various density: broad-flung jets of steam, coldly white against the murky distance; wan smoke from lime-kilns, wafted in long trails; reek of solid blackness from pits and forges, voluming aloft and far-floated by the sluggish wind.

Born at Birmingham, the son of a teacher of drawing, Maurice Hilliard had spent most of his life in the Midland capital; to its grammar school he owed an education just sufficiently prolonged to unfit him for the tasks of an underling, yet not thorough enough to qualify him for professional life. In boyhood he aspired to the career of an artist, but his father, himself the wreck of a would-be painter, rudely discouraged this ambition; by way of compromise between the money-earning craft and the beggarly art, he became a mechanical-draughtsman. Of late years he had developed a strong taste for the study of architecture; much of his leisure was given to this subject, and what money he could spare went in the purchase of books and prints which helped him to extend his architectural knowledge. In moods of hope, he had asked himself whether it might not be possible to escape from bondage to the gods of iron, and earn a living in an architect's office. That desire was now forgotten in his passionate resolve to enjoy liberty without regard for the future.

All his possessions, save the articles of clothing which he would carry with him, were packed in a couple of trunks, to be sent on the morrow to Birmingham, where they would lie in the care of his friend Narramore. Kinsfolk he had none whom he cared to remember, except his sister; she lived at Wolverhampton, a wife and mother, in narrow but not oppressive circumstances, and Hilliard had taken leave of her in a short visit some days ago. He would not wait for the wedding of his sister-in-law; enough that she was provided for, and that his conscience would always be at ease on her account.

For he was troubled with a conscience—even with one unusually poignant. An anecdote from his twentieth year depicts this feature of the man. He and Narramore were walking one night in a very poor part of Birmingham, and for some reason they chanced to pause by a shop-window—a small window, lighted with one gas-jet, and laid out with a miserable handful of paltry wares; the shop, however, was newly opened, and showed a pathetic attempt at cleanliness and neatness. The friends asked each other how it could possibly benefit anyone to embark in such a business as that, and laughed over the display. While he was laughing, Hilliard became aware of a woman in the doorway, evidently the shopkeeper; she had heard their remarks and looked distressed. Infinitely keener was the pang which Maurice experienced; he could not forgive himself, kept exclaiming how brutally he had behaved, and sank into gloominess. Not very long after, he took Narramore to walk in the same direction; they came again to the little shop, and Hilliard surprised his companion with a triumphant shout. The window was now laid out in a much more promising way, with goods of modest value. "You remember?" said the young man. "I couldn't rest till I had sent her something. She'll wonder to the end of her life who the money came from. But she's made use of it, poor creature, and it'll bring her luck."

Only the hopeless suppression of natural desires, the conflict through years of ardent youth with sordid circumstances, could have brought him to the pass he had now reached—one of desperation centred in self. Every suggestion of native suavity and prudence was swept away in tumultuous revolt. Another twelvemonth of his slavery and he would have yielded to brutalising influences which rarely relax their hold upon a man. To-day he was prompted by the instinct of flight from peril threatening all that was worthy in him.

Just as the last glimmer of daylight vanished from his room there sounded a knock at the door.

"Your tea's ready, Mr. Hilliard," called a woman's voice.

He took his meals downstairs in the landlady's parlour. Appetite at present he had none, but the pretence of eating was a way of passing the time; so he descended and sat down at the prepared table.

His wandering eyes fell on one of the ornaments of the room—Mrs. Brewer's album. On first coming to live in the house, two years ago, he had examined this collection of domestic portraits, and subsequently, from time to time, had taken up the album to look at one photograph which interested him. Among an assemblage of types excelling in ugliness of feature and hideousness of costume—types of toil-worn age, of ungainly middle life, and of youth lacking every grace, such as are exhibited in the albums of the poor—there was discoverable one female portrait in which, the longer he gazed at it, Hilliard found an ever-increasing suggestiveness of those qualities he desired in woman. Unclasping the volume, he opened immediately at this familiar face. A month or two had elapsed since he last regarded it, and the countenance took possession of him with the same force as ever.

It was that of a young woman probably past her twentieth year. Unlike her neighbours in the album, she had not bedizened herself before sitting to be portrayed. The abundant hair was parted simply and smoothly from her forehead and tightly plaited behind; she wore a linen collar, and, so far as could be judged from the portion included in the picture, a homely cloth gown. Her features were comely and intelligent, and exhibited a gentleness, almost a meekness of expression which was as far as possible from seeming affected. Whether she smiled or looked sad Hilliard had striven vainly to determine. Her lips appeared to smile, but in so slight a degree that perchance it was merely an effect of natural line; whereas, if the mouth were concealed, a profound melancholy at once ruled the visage.

Who she was Hilliard had no idea. More than once he had been on the point of asking his landlady, but characteristic delicacies restrained him: he feared Mrs. Brewer's mental comment, and dreaded the possible disclosure that he had admired a housemaid or someone of yet lower condition. Nor could he trust his judgment of the face: perhaps it shone only by contrast with so much ugliness on either side of it; perhaps, in the starved condition of his senses, he was ready to find perfection in any female countenance not frankly repulsive.

Yet, no; it was a beautiful face. Beautiful, at all events, in the sense of being deeply interesting, in the strength of its appeal to his emotions. Another man might pass it slightingly; to him it spoke as no

other face had ever spoken. It awakened in him a consciousness of profound sympathy.

While he still sat at table his landlady came in. She was a worthy
woman of her class, not given to vulgar gossip. Her purpose in entering the room at this moment was to ask Hilliard whether he had a
likeness of himself which he could spare her, as a memento.

"I'm sorry I don't possess such a thing," he answered, laughing,
surprised that the woman should care enough about him to make the
request. "But, talking of photographs, would you tell me who this
is?"

The album lay beside him, and a feeling of embarrassment, as he
saw Mrs. Brewer's look rest upon it, impelled him to the decisive
question.

"That? Oh! that's a friend of my daughter Martha's—Eve
Madeley. I'm sure I don't wonder at you noticing her. But it doesn't
do her justice; she's better looking than that. It was took better than
two years ago—why, just before you came to me, Mr. Hilliard. She
was going away—to London."

"Eve Madeley." He repeated the name to himself, and liked it.

"She's had a deal of trouble, poor thing," pursued the landlady.
"We was sorry to lose sight of her, but glad, I'm sure, that she went
away to do better for herself. She hasn't been home since then, and we
don't hear of her comimg, and I'm sure nobody can be surprised. But
our Martha heard from her not so long ago—why, it was about
Christmas-time."

"Is she"—he was about to add, "in service?" but could not voice
the words. "She has an engagement in London?"

"Yes; she's a bookkeeper, and earns her pound a week. She was
always clever at figures. She got on so well at the school that they
wanted her to be a teacher, but she didn't like it. Then Mr. Reckitt,
the ironmonger, a friend of her father's, got her to help him with his
books and bills of an evening, and when she was seventeen, because
his business was growing and he hadn't much of a head for figures
himself, he took her regular into the shop. And glad she was to give
up the school-teaching, for she could never abear it."

"You say she had a lot of trouble?"

"Ah, that indeed she had! And all her father's fault. But for him,
foolish man, they might have been a well-to-do family. But he's had to
suffer for it himself, too. He lives up here on the hill, in a poor cottage, and takes wages as a timekeeper at Robinson's when he ought to
have been paying men of his own. The drink—that's what it was.
When our Martha first knew them they were living at Walsall, and if
it hadn't a'been for Eve they'd have had no home at all. Martha got to

know her at the Sunday-school; Eve used to teach a class. That's seven
or eight years ago; she was only a girl of sixteen, but she had the ways
of a grown-up woman, and very lucky it was for them belonging to
her. Often and often they've gone for days with nothing but a dry loaf,
and the father spending all he got at the public."

"Was it a large family?" Hilliard inquired.

"Well, let me see; at that time there was Eve's two sisters and her
brother. Two other children had died, and the mother was dead, too. I
don't know much about *her*, but they say she was a very good sort of
woman, and it's likely the eldest girl took after her. A quieter and
modester girl than Eve there never was. Our Martha lived with her
aunt at Walsall—that's my only sister, and she was bed-rid, poor
thing, and had Martha to look after her. And when she died, and
Martha came back here to us, the Madeley family came here as well,
'cause the father got some kind of work. But he couldn't keep it, and
he went off I don't know where, and Eve had the children to keep and
look after. We used to do what we could to help her, but it was a cruel
life for a poor thing of her age—just when she ought to have been
enjoying her life, as you may say."

Hilliard's interest waxed.

"Then," pursued Mrs. Brewer, "the next sister to Eve, Laura her
name was, went to Birmingham, into a sweetstuff shop, and that was
the last ever seen or heard of her. She wasn't a girl to be depended
upon, and I never thought she'd come to good, and whether she's alive
or dead there's no knowing. Eve took it to heart, that she did. And not
six months after, the other girl had the 'sipelas, and she died, and just
as they was carrying her coffin out of the house, who should come up
but her father! He'd been away for nearly two years, just sending a
little money now and then, and he didn't even know the girl had been
ailing. And when he saw the coffin, it took him so that he fell down
just like a dead man. You wouldn't have thought it, but there's no
knowing what goes on in people's minds. Well, if you'll believe it,
from that day he was so changed we didn't seem to know him. He
turned quite religious, and went regular to chapel, and has done ever
since; and he wouldn't touch a drop of anything, tempt him who
might. It was a case of conversion, if ever there was one."

"So there remained only Eve and her brother?"

"Yes. He was a steady lad, Tom Madeley, and never gave his sister
much trouble. He earns his thirty shillings a week now. Well, and
soon after she saw her father going on all right, Eve left home. I don't
wonder at it; it wasn't to be expected she could forgive him for all the
harm and sorrows he'd caused. She went to Birmingham for a few
months, and then she came back one day to tell us she'd got a place in
London. And she brought that photo to give us to remember her by.

But, as I said, it isn't good enough."

"Does she seem to be happier now?"

"She hasn't wrote more than once or twice, but she's doing well, and whatever happens she's not the one to complain. It's a blessing she's always had her health. No doubt she's made friends in London, but we haven't heard about them. Martha was hoping she'd have come for Christmas, but it seems she couldn't get away for long enough from business. I'd tell you her address, but I don't remember it. I've never been in London myself. Martha knows it, of course. She might look in to-night, and if she does I'll ask her."

Hilliard allowed this suggestion to pass without remark. He was not quite sure that he desired to know Miss Madeley's address.

But later in the evening, when, after walking for two or three hours about the cold, dark roads, he came in to have his supper and go to bed, Mrs. Brewer smilingly offered him a scrap of paper.

"There," she said, "that's where she's living. London's a big place, and you mayn't be anywhere near, but if you happened to walk that way, we should take it kindly if you'd just leave word that we're always glad to hear from her, and hope she's well."

With a mixture of reluctance and satisfaction the young man took the paper, glanced at it, and folded it to put in his pocket. Mrs. Brewer was regarding him, and he felt that his silence must seem ungracious.

"I will certainly call and leave your message," he said.

Up in his bed-room he sat for a long time with the paper lying open before him. And when he slept his rest was troubled with dreams of an anxious search about the highways and byways of London for that half-sad, half-smiling face which had so wrought upon his imagination.

Long before daylight he awoke at the sound of bells, and hootings, and whistlings, which summoned the Dudley workfolk to their labour. For the first time in his life he heard these hideous noises with pleasure: they told him that the day of his escape had come. Unable to lie still, he rose at once, and went out into the chill dawn. Thoughts of Eve Madeley no longer possessed him; a glorious sense of freedom excluded every recollection of his past life, and he wandered aimlessly with a song in his heart.

At breakfast, the sight of Mrs. Brewer's album tempted him to look once more at the portrait, but he did not yield.

"Shall we ever see you again, I wonder?" asked his landlady, when the moment arrived for leave-taking.

"If I am ever again in Dudley, I shall come here," he answered kindly.

But on his way to the station he felt a joyful assurance that fate would have no power to draw him back again into this circle of fiery torments.

## CHAPTER V

Two months later, on a brilliant morning of May, Hilliard again awoke from troubled dreams, but the sounds about him had no association with bygone miseries. From the courtyard upon which his window looked there came a ringing of gay laughter followed by shrill, merry gossip in a foreign tongue. Somewhere in the neighbourhood a church bell was pealing. Presently footsteps hurried along the corridor, and an impatient voice shouted repeatedly, "Alphonse! Alphonse!"

He was in Paris; had been there for six weeks, and now awoke with a sense of loneliness, a desire to be back among his own people.

In London he had spent only a fortnight. It was not a time that he cared to reflect upon. No sooner had he found himself in the metropolis, alone and free, with a pocketful of money, than a delirium possessed him. Every resolution notwithstanding, he yielded to London's grossest lures. All he could remember, was a succession of extravagances, beneath a sunless sky, with chance companions whose faces he had forgotten five minutes after parting with them. Sovereign after sovereign melted out of his hand; the end of the second week found his capital diminished by some five-and-twenty pounds. In an hour of physical and moral nausea, he packed his travelling-bag, journeyed to Newhaven, and as a sort of penance, crossed the Channel by third-class passage. Arrived in Paris, he felt himself secure, and soon recovered sanity.

Thanks to his studious habits, he was equipped with book-French; now, both for economy's sake and for his mental advantage, he struggled with the spoken language, and so far succeeded as to lodge very cheaply in a rather disreputable hotel, and to eat at restaurants where dinner of several courses cost two francs and a half. His life was irreproachable; he studied the Paris of art and history. But perforce he remained companionless, and solitude had begun to weigh upon him.

This morning, whilst he sat over his bowl of coffee and *petit pain*, a certain recollection haunted him persistently. Yesterday, in turning out his pockets, he had come upon a scrap of paper, whereon was written:

93, Belmont Street, Chalk Farm Road, London, N.W.

This formula it was which now kept running through his mind, like a refrain which will not be dismissed.

He reproached himself for neglect of his promise to Mrs. Brewer. More than that, he charged himself with foolish disregard of a possibility which might have boundless significance for him. Here, it seemed, was sufficient motive for a return to London. The alternative was to wander on, and see more of foreign countries; a tempting suggestion, but marred by the prospect of loneliness. He would go back among his own people and make friends. Without comradeship, liberty had little savour.

Still travelling with as small expense as might be, he reached London in the forenoon, left his luggage at Victoria Station, and, after a meal, betook himself in the northerly direction. It was a rainy and uncomfortable day, but this did not much affect his spirits; he felt like a man new risen from illness, seemed to have cast off something that had threatened his very existence, and marvelled at the state of mind in which it had been possible for him to inhabit London without turning his steps towards the address of Eve Madeley.

He discovered Belmont Street. It consisted of humble houses, and was dreary enough to look upon. As he sought for No. 93, a sudden nervousness attacked him; he became conscious all at once of the strangeness of his position. At this hour it was unlikely that Eve would be at home; an inquiry at the house and the leaving of a verbal message would discharge his obligation; but he proposed more than that. It was his resolve to see Eve herself, to behold the face which, in a picture, had grown so familiar to him. Yet till this moment he had overlooked the difficulties of the enterprise. Could he, on the strength of an acquaintance with Mrs. Brewer, claim the friendly regards of this girl who had never heard his name? If he saw her once, on what pretext could he seek for a second meeting?

Possibly he would not desire it. Eve in her own person might disenchant him.

Meanwhile he had discovered the house, and without further debate he knocked. The door was opened by a woman of ordinary type, slatternly, and with suspicious eye.

"Miss Madeley *did* live here," she said, "but she's been gone a month or more."

"Can you tell me where she is living now?"

After a searching look the woman replied that she could not. In the manner of her kind, she was anxious to dismiss the inquirer and get the door shut. Gravely disappointed, Hilliard felt unable to turn away without a further question.

"Perhaps you know where she is, or was, employed?"

But no information whatever was forthcoming. It very rarely is under such circumstances, for a London landlady, compounded in general of craft and caution, tends naturally to reticence on the score of her former lodgers. If she has parted with them on amicable terms, her instinct is to shield them against the menace presumed in every inquiry; if her mood is one of ill-will, she refuses information lest the departed should reap advantage. And then, in the great majority of cases she has really no information to give.

The door closed with that severity of exclusion in which London doors excel, and Hilliard turned despondently away. He was just consoling himself with the thought that Eve would probably, before long, communicate her new address to the friends at Dudley, and by that means he might hear of it, when a dirty-faced little girl, who had stood within ear-shot while he was talking, and who had followed him to the end of the street, approached him with an abrupt inquiry.

"Was you asking for Miss Madeley, Sir?"

"Yes, I was; do you know anything of her?"

"My mother did washing for her, and when she moved I had to take some things of hers to the new address."

"Then you remember it?"

"It's a goodish way from 'ere, Sir. Shall I go with you?"

Hilliard understood. Like the good Samaritan of old, he took out twopence. The face of the dirty little girl brightened wonderfully.

"Tell me the address; that will be enough."

"Do you know Gower Place, Sir?"

"Somewhere near Gower Street, I suppose?"

His supposition was confirmed, and he learnt the number of the house to which Miss Madeley had transferred herself. In that direction he at once bent his steps.

Gower Place is in the close neighbourhood of Euston Road; Hilliard remembered that he had passed the end of it on his first arrival in London, when he set forth from Euston Station to look for a lodging. It was a mere chance that he had not turned into this very street, instead of going further. Several windows displayed lodging-cards. On the whole, it looked a better locality than Belmont Street. Eve's removal hither might signify an improvement of circumstances.

The house which he sought had a clean doorstep and unusually bright windows. His knock was answered quickly, and by a young, sprightly woman, who smiled upon him.

"I believe Miss Madeley lives here?"

"Yes, she does."

"She is not at home just now?"

"No. She went out after breakfast, and I'm sure I can't say when she'll be back."

Hilliard felt a slight wonder at this uncertainty. The young woman, observing his expression, added with vivacious friendliness:

"Do you want to see her on business?"

"No; a private matter."

This occasioned a smirk.

"Well, she hasn't any regular hours at present. Sometimes she comes to dinner, sometimes she doesn't. Sometimes she comes to tea, but just as often she isn't 'ome till late. P'r'aps you'd like to leave your name?"

"I think I'll call again."

"Did you expect to find her at 'ome now?" asked the young woman, whose curiosity grew more eager as she watched Hilliard's countenance.

"Perhaps," he replied, neglecting the question, "I should find her here to-morrow morning?"

"Well, I can say as someone's going to call, you know."

"Please do so."

Therewith he turned away, anxious to escape a volley of interrogation for which the landlady's tongue was primed.

He walked into Gower Street, and pondered the awkward interview that now lay before him. On his calling to-morrow, Miss Madeley would doubtless come to speak with him at the door; even supposing she had a parlour at her disposal, she was not likely to invite a perfect stranger into the house. How could he make her acquaintance on the doorstep? To be sure, he brought a message, but this commission had been so long delayed that he felt some shame about discharging it. In any case, his delivery of the message would sound odd; there would be embarrassment on both sides.

Why was Eve so uncertain in her comings and goings? Necessity of business, perhaps. Yet he had expected quite the opposite state of things. From Mrs. Brewer's description of the girl's character, he had imagined her leading a life of clockwork regularity. The point was very trivial, but it somehow caused a disturbance of his thoughts, which tended to misgiving.

In the meantime he had to find quarters for himself. Why not seek them in Gower Place?

After ten minutes' sauntering, he retraced his steps, and walked down the side of the street opposite to that on which Eve's lodgings were situated. Nearly over against that particular house was a window with a card. Carelessly he approached the door, and carelessly asked to see the rooms that were to let. They were comfortless, but would suit his purpose for a time. He engaged a sitting-room on the ground-floor, and a bed-room above, and went to fetch his luggage from Victoria Station.

On the steamer last night he had not slept, and now that he was once more housed, an overpowering fatigue constrained him to lie down and close his eyes. Almost immediately he fell into oblivion, and lay sleeping on the cranky sofa, until the entrance of a girl with tea-things awakened him.

From his parlour window he could very well observe the houses opposite without fear of drawing attention from anyone on that side; and so it happened that, without deliberate purpose of espial, he watched the door of Eve Madeley's residence for a long time; till, in fact, he grew weary of the occupation. No one had entered; no one had come forth. At half-past seven he took his hat and left the house.

Scarcely had he closed the door behind him when he became aware that a lightly tripping and rather showily dressed girl, who was coming down the other side of the way, had turned off the pavement and was plying the knocker at the house which interested him. He gazed eagerly. Impossible that a young person of that garb and deportment should be Eve Madeley. Her face was hidden from him, and at this distance he could not have recognised the features, even presuming that his familiarity with the portrait, taken more than two years ago, would enable him to identify Eve when he saw her. The door opened; the girl was admitted. Afraid of being noticed, he walked on.

The distance to the head of the street was not more than thirty yards; there lay Gower Street, on the right hand the Metropolitan station, to the left a long perspective southwards. Delaying in doubt as to his course, Hilliard glanced back. From the house which attracted his eyes he saw come forth the girl who had recently entered, and close following her another young woman. They began to walk sharply towards where he stood.

He did not stir, and the couple drew so near that he could observe their faces. In the second girl he recognised—or believed that he recognised—Eve Madeley.

She wore a costume in decidedly better taste than her companion's; for all that, her appearance struck him as quite unlike that he would have expected Eve Madeley to present. He had thought of her as very plainly, perhaps poorly, clad; but this attire was ornate, and looked rather expensive; it might be in the mode of the new season. In figure, she was altogether a more imposing young woman than he had pictured to himself. His pulses were sensibly quickened as he looked at her.

The examination was of necessity hurried. Walking at a sharp pace, they rapidly came close to where he stood. He drew aside to let them pass, and at that moment caught a few words of their conversation.

"I told you we should be late," exclaimed the unknown girl, in friendly remonstrance.

"What does it matter?" replied Eve—if Eve it were. "I hate standing at the doors. We shall find seats somewhere."

Her gay, careless tones astonished the listener. Involuntarily he began to follow; but at the edge of the pavement in Gower Street they stopped, and by advancing another step or two he distinctly overheard the continuation of their talk.

"The 'bus will take a long time."

"Bother the 'bus!" This was Eve Madeley again—if Eve it could really be. "We'll have a cab. Look, there's a crawler in Euston Road. I've stopped him!"

"I say, Eve, you *are* going it!"

This exclamation from the other girl was the last sentence that fell on Hilliard's ear. They both tripped off towards the cab which Eve's gesture had summoned. He saw them jump in and drive away.

"I say, Eve, you *are* going it!" Why, there his doubt was settled; the name confirmed him in his identification. But he stood motionless with astonishment.

They were going to a theatre, of course. And Eve spoke as if money were of no consequence to her. She had the look, the tones, of one bent on enjoying herself, of one who habitually pursued pleasure, and that in its most urban forms.

Her companion had a voice of thinner quality, of higher note, which proclaimed a subordinate character. It sounded, moreover, with the London accent, while Eve's struck a more familiar note to the man of the Midlands. Eve seemed to be the elder of the two; it could not be thought for a moment that her will was guided by that of the more trivial girl.

Eve Madeley—the meek, the melancholy, the long-suffering, the pious—what did it all mean?

Utterly bewildered, the young man walked on without thought of direction, and rambled dreamily about the streets for an hour or two. He could not make up his mind whether or not to fulfil the promise of calling to see Miss Madeley to-morrow morning. At one moment he regretted having taken lodgings in Gower Place; at another he determined to make use of his advantage, and play the spy upon Eve's movements without scruple. The interest she had hitherto excited in him was faint indeed compared with emotions such as this first glimpse of her had kindled and fanned. A sense of peril warned him to hold aloof; tumult of his senses rendered the warning useless.

At eleven o'clock he was sitting by his bedroom window, in darkness, watching the house across the way.


# CHAPTER VI

It was just upon midnight when Eve returned. She came at a quick walk, and alone; the light of the street-lamps showed her figure distinctly enough to leave the watcher in no doubt. A latchkey admitted her to the house. Presently there appeared a light at an upper window, and a shadow kept moving across the blind. When the light was extinguished Hilliard went to bed, but that night he slept little.

The next morning passed in restless debate with himself. He did not cross the way to call upon Eve: the thought of speaking with her on the doorstep of a lodging-house proved intolerable. All day long he kept his post of observation. Other persons he saw leave and enter the house, but Miss Madeley did not come forth. That he could have missed her seemed impossible, for even while eating his meals he remained by the window. Perchance she had left home very early in the morning, but it was unlikely.

Through the afternoon it rained: the gloomy sky intensified his fatigue and despondence. About six o'clock, exhausted in mind and body, he had allowed his attention to stray, when the sudden clang of a street organ startled him. His eyes turned in the wonted direction—and instantly he sprang up. To clutch his hat, to rush from the room and from the house, occupied but a moment. There, walking away on the other side, was Eve. Her fawn-coloured mantle, her hat with the yellow flowers, were the same as yesterday. The rain had ceased; in the western sky appeared promise of a fair evening.

Hilliard pursued her in a parallel line. At the top of the street she crossed towards him; he let her pass by and followed closely. She entered the booking-office of Gower Street station; he drew as near as possible and heard her ask for a ticket——

"Healtheries; third return."

The slang term for the Health Exhibition at Kensington was familiar to him from the English papers he had seen in Paris. As soon as Eve had passed on he obtained a like ticket and hastened down the steps in pursuit. A minute or two and he was sitting face to face with her in the railway carriage.

He could now observe her at his leisure and compare her features with those represented in the photograph. Mrs. Brewer had said truly that the portrait did not do her justice; he saw the resemblance, yet what a difference between the face he had brooded over at Dudley and that which lived before him! A difference not to be accounted for by mere lapse of time. She could not, he thought, have changed greatly in the last two or three years, for her age at the time of sitting for the photograph must have been at least one-and-twenty. She did not look older than he had expected: it was still a young face, but—and herein he found its strangeness—that of a woman who views life without embarrassment, without anxiety. She sat at her ease, casting careless glances this way and that. When her eyes fell upon him he winced, yet she paid no more heed to him than to the other passengers.

Presently she became lost in thought; her eyes fell. Ah! now the resemblance to the portrait came out more distinctly. Her lips shaped themselves to that expression which he knew so well, the half-smile telling of habitual sadness.

His fixed gaze recalled her to herself, and immediately the countenance changed beyond recognition. Her eyes wandered past him with a look of cold if not defiant reserve; the lips lost all their sweetness. He was chilled with vague distrust, and once again asked himself whether this could be the Eve Madeley whose history he had heard.

Again she fell into abstraction, and some trouble seemed to grow upon her mind. It was difficult now to identify her with the girl who had talked and laughed so gaily last evening. Towards the end of the journey a nervous restlessness began to appear in her looks and movements. Hilliard felt that he had annoyed her by the persistency of his observation, and tried to keep his eyes averted. But no; the disturbance she betrayed was due to some other cause; probably she paid not the least regard to him.

At Earl's Court she alighted hurriedly. By this time Hilliard had begun to feel shame in the ignoble part he was playing, but choice he had none—the girl drew him irresistibly to follow and watch her. Among the crowd entering the Exhibition he could easily keep her in sight without risk of his espial being detected. That Eve had come to keep an appointment with some acquaintance he felt sure, and at any cost he must discover who the person was.

The event justified him with unexpected suddenness. No sooner had she passed the turnstile than a man stepped forward, saluting her in form. Eve shook hands with him, and they walked on.

Uncontrollable wrath seized on Hilliard and shook him from head to foot. A meeting of this kind was precisely what he had foreseen, and he resented it violently.

Eve's acquaintance had the external attributes of a gentleman. One could not easily imagine him a clerk or a shop-assistant smartened up for the occasion. He was plain of feature, but wore a pleasant, honest look, and his demeanour to the girl showed not only good breeding but unmistakable interest of the warmest kind. His age might perhaps be thirty; he was dressed well, and in all respects conventionally.

In Eve's behaviour there appeared a very noticeable reserve; she rarely turned her face to him while he spoke, and seemed to make only the briefest remarks. Her attention was given to the objects they passed.

Totally unconscious of the scenes through which he was moving, Hilliard tracked the couple for more than an hour. He noticed that the man once took out his watch, and from this trifling incident he sought to derive a hope; perhaps Eve would be quit ere long of the detested companionship. They came at length to where a band was playing, and sat down on chairs; the pursuer succeeded in obtaining a seat behind them, but the clamour of instruments overpowered their voices, or rather the man's voice, for Eve seemed not to speak at all. One moment, when her neighbour's head approached nearer than usual to hers, she drew slightly away.

The music ceased, whereupon Eve's companion again consulted his watch.

"It's a most unfortunate thing." He was audible now. "I can't possibly stay longer."

Eve moved on her chair, as if in readiness to take leave of him, but she did not speak.

"You think it likely you will meet Miss Ringrose?"

Eve answered, but the listener could not catch her words.

"I'm so very sorry. If there had been any——"

The voice sank, and Hilliard could only gather from observance of the man's face that he was excusing himself in fervent tones for the necessity of departure. Then they both rose and walked a few yards together. Finally, with a sense of angry exultation, Hilliard saw them part.

For a little while Eve stood watching the musicians, who were making ready to play a new piece. As soon as the first note sounded she moved slowly, her eyes cast down. With fiercely throbbing heart, thinking and desiring and hoping he knew not what, Hilliard once more followed her. Night had now fallen; the grounds of the Exhibition shone with many-coloured illumination; the throng grew dense. It was both easy and necessary to keep very near to the object of his interest.

There sounded a clinking of plates, cups, and glasses. People were sitting at tables in the open air, supplied with refreshments by the waiters who hurried hither and thither. Eve, after a show of hesitation, took a seat by a little round table which stood apart; her pursuer found a place whence he could keep watch. She gave an order, and presently there was brought to her a glass of wine with a sandwich.

Hilliard called for a bottle of ale: he was consumed with thirst.

"Dare I approach her?" he asked himself. "Is it possible? And, if possible, is it any use?"

The difficulty was to explain his recognition of her. But for that, he might justify himself in addressing her.

She had finished her wine and was looking round. Her glance fell upon him, and for a moment rested. With a courage not his own, Hilliard rose, advanced, and respectfully doffed his hat.

"Miss Madeley——"

The note was half interrogative, but his voice failed before he could add another syllable. Eve drew herself up, rigid in the alarm of female instinct.

"I am a stranger to you," Hilliard managed to say. "But I come from Dudley; I know some of your friends——"

His hurried words fell into coherence. At the name "Dudley" Eve's features relaxed.

"Was it you who called at my lodgings the day before yesterday?"

"I did. Your address was given me by Mrs. Brewer, in whose house I have lived for a long time. She wished me to call and to give you a kind message—to say how glad they would be to hear from you——"

"But you *didn't* leave the message."

The smile put Hilliard at his ease, it was so gentle and friendly.

"I wasn't able to come at the time I mentioned. I should have called to-morrow."

"But how is it that you knew me? I think," she added, without waiting for a reply, "that I have seen you somewhere. But I can't remember where."

"Perhaps in the train this evening?"

"Yes; so it was. You knew me then?"

"I thought I did, for I happened to come out from my lodgings at the moment you were leaving yours, just opposite, and we walked almost together to Gower Street station. I must explain that I have taken rooms in Gower Place. I didn't like to speak to you in the street; but now that I have again chanced to see you——"

"I still don't understand," said Eve, who was speaking with the most perfect ease of manner. "I am not the only person living in that house. Why should you take it for granted that I was Miss Madeley?"

Hilliard had not ventured to seat himself; he stood before her, head respectfully bent.

"At Mrs. Brewer's I saw your portrait."

Her eyes fell.

"My portrait. You really could recognise me from that?"

"Oh, readily! Will you allow me to sit down?"

"Of course. I shall be glad to hear the news you have brought. I couldn't imagine who it was had called and wanted to see me. But there's another thing. I didn't think Mrs. Brewer knew my address. I have moved since I wrote to her daughter."

"No; it was the old address she gave me. I ought to have mentioned that: it escaped my mind. First of all I went to Belmont Street."

"Mysteries still!" exclaimed Eve. "The people *there* couldn't know where I had gone to."

"A child who had carried some parcel for you to Gower Place volunteered information."

Outwardly amused, and bearing herself as though no incident could easily disconcert her, Eve did not succeed in suppressing every sign of nervousness. Constrained by his wonder to study her with critical attention, the young man began to feel assured that she was consciously acting a part. That she should be able to carry it off so well, therein lay the marvel. Of course, London had done much for her. Possessing no common gifts, she must have developed remarkably under changed conditions, and might, indeed, have become a very different person from the country girl who toiled to support her drunken father's family. Hilliard remembered the mention of her sister who had gone to Birmingham and disappeared; it suggested a characteristic of the Madeley blood, which possibly must be borne in mind if he would interpret Eve.

She rested her arms on the little round table.

"So Mrs. Brewer asked you to come and find me?"

"It was only a suggestion, and I may as well tell you how it came about. I used to have my meals in Mrs. Brewer's parlour, and to amuse myself I looked over her album. There I found your portrait, and—well, it interested me, and I asked the name of the original."

Hilliard was now in command of himself; he spoke with simple directness, as his desires dictated.

"And Mrs. Brewer," said Eve, with averted eyes, "told you about me?"

"She spoke of you as her daughter's friend," was the evasive answer. Eve seemed to accept it as sufficient, and there was a long silence.

"My name is Hilliard," the young man resumed. "I am taking the first holiday, worth speaking of, that I have known for a good many years. At Dudley my business was to make mechanical drawings, and I can't say that I enjoyed the occupation."

"Are you going back to it?"

"Not just yet. I have been in France, and I may go abroad again before long."

"For your pleasure?" Eve asked, with interest.

"To answer 'Yes' wouldn't quite express what I mean. I am learning to live."

She hastily searched his face for the interpretation of these words, then looked away, with grave, thoughtful countenance.

"By good fortune," Hilliard pursued. "I have become possessed of money enough to live upon for a year or two. At the end of it I may find myself in the old position, and have to be a living machine once more. But I shall be able to remember that I was once a man."

Eve regarded him strangely, with wide, intent eyes, as though his speech had made a peculiar impression upon her.

"Can you see any sense in that?" he asked, smiling.

"Yes. I think I understand you."

She spoke slowly, and Hilliard, watching her, saw in her face more of the expression of her portrait than he had yet discovered. Her soft tone was much more like what he had expected to hear than her utterances hitherto.

"Have you always lived at Dudley?" she asked.

He sketched rapidly the course of his life, without reference to domestic circumstances. Before he had ceased speaking he saw that Eve's look was directed towards something at a distance behind him; she smiled, and at length nodded, in recognition of some person who approached. Then a voice caused him to look round.

"Oh, there you are! I have been hunting for you ever so long."

As soon as Hilliard saw the speaker, he had no difficulty in remembering her. It was Eve's companion of the day before yesterday, with whom she had started for the theatre. The girl evidently felt some surprise at discovering her friend in conversation with a man she did not know; but Eve was equal to the situation, and spoke calmly.

"This gentleman is from my part of the world—from Dudley. Mr. Hilliard—Miss Ringrose."

Hilliard stood up. Miss Ringrose, after attempting a bow of formal dignity, jerked out her hand, gave a shy little laugh, and said with amusing abruptness—

"Do you really come from Dudley?"

"I do really, Miss Ringrose. Why does it sound strange to you?"

"Oh, I don't mean that it sounds strange." She spoke in a high but not unmusical note, very quickly, and with timid glances to either side of her collocutor. "But Eve—Miss Madeley—gave me the idea that Dudley people must be great, rough, sooty men. Don't laugh at me, please. You know very well, Eve, that you always talk in that way. Of course, I knew that there must be people of a different kind, but— there now, you're making me confused, and I don't know what I meant to say."

She was a thin-faced, but rather pretty girl, with auburn hair. Belonging to a class which, especially in its women, has little intelligence to boast of, she yet redeemed herself from the charge of commonness by a certain vivacity of feature and an agreeable sugges- tion of good feeling in her would-be frank but nervous manner. Hilliard laughed merrily at the vision in her mind of "great, rough, sooty men."

"I'm sorry to disappoint you, Miss Ringrose."

"No, but really—what sort of a place *is* Dudley? Is it true that they call it the Black Country?"

"Let us walk about," interposed Eve. "Mr. Hilliard will tell you all he can about the Black Country."

She moved on, and they rambled aimlessly; among cigar-smoking clerks and shopmen, each with the female of his kind in wondrous hat and drapery; among domestic groups from the middle-class suburbs, and from regions of the artisan; among the frankly rowdy and the solemnly superior; here and there a man in evening dress, generally conscious of his white tie and starched shirt, and a sprinkling of unattached young women with roving eyes. Hilliard, excited by the success of his advances, and by companionship after long solitude, became very unlike himself, talking and jesting freely. Most of the conversation passed between him and Miss Ringrose; Eve had fallen into an absent mood, answered carelessly when addressed, laughed without genuine amusement, and sometimes wore the look of trouble which Hilliard had observed whilst in the train.

Before long she declared that it was time to go home.

"What's the hurry?" said her friend. "It's nothing like ten o'clock yet—is it, Mr. Hilliard?"

"I don't wish to stay any longer. Of course you needn't go unless you like, Patty."

Hilliard had counted on travelling back with her; to his great disappointment, Eve answered his request to be allowed to do so with a coldly civil refusal which there was no misunderstanding.

"But I hope you will let me see you again?"

"As you live so near me," she answered, "we are pretty sure to meet. Are you coming or not, Patty?"

"Oh, of course I shall go if you do."

The young man shook hands with them; rather formally with Eve, with Patty Ringrose as cordially as if they were old friends. And then he lost sight of them amid the throng.


## CHAPTER VII

How did Eve Madeley contrive to lead this life of leisure and amusement? The question occupied Hilliard well on into the small hours; he could hit upon no explanation which had the least plausibility.

Was she engaged to be married to the man who met her at the Exhibition? Her behaviour in his company by no means supported such a surmise; yet there must be something more than ordinary acquaintance between the two.

Might not Patty Ringrose be able and willing to solve for him the riddle of Eve's existence? But he had no idea where Patty lived. He recalled her words in Gower Street: "You *are* going it, Eve!" and they stirred miserable doubts; yet something more than mere hope inclined him to believe that the girl's life was innocent. Her look, her talk reassured him; so did her friendship with such a person as the ingenuous Patty. On learning that he dwelt close by her she gave no sign of an uneasy conscience.

In any case, the contrast between her actual life and that suggested by Mrs. Brewer's talk about her was singular enough. It supplied him with a problem of which the interest would not easily be exhausted. But he must pursue the study with due regard to honour and delicacy; he would act the spy no more. As Eve had said, they were pretty sure to meet before long; if his patience failed it was always possible for him to write a letter.

Four days went by and he saw nothing of her. On the fifth, as he was walking homeward in the afternoon, he came face to face with Miss Madeley in Gower Street. She stopped at once, and offered a friendly hand.

"Will you let me walk a little way with you?" he asked.

"Certainly. I'm just going to change a book at Mudie's." She carried a little handbag. "I suppose you have been going about London a great deal? Don't the streets look beautiful at this time of the year?"

"Beautiful? I'm not sure that I see much beauty."

"Oh, don't you? I delight in London. I had dreamt of it all my life before I came here. I always said to myself I should some day live in London."

Her voice to-day had a vibrant quality which seemed to result from some agreeable emotion. Hilliard remarked a gleam in her eyes and a colour in her cheeks which gave her an appearance of better health than a few days ago.

"You never go into the country?" he said, feeling unable to join in her praise of London, though it was intelligible enough to him.

"I go now and then as far as Hampstead Heath," Eve answered with a smile. "If it's fine I shall be there next Sunday with Patty Ringrose."

Hilliard grasped the opportunity. Would she permit him to meet her and Miss Ringrose at Hampstead? Without shadow of constraint or affectation, Eve replied that such a meeting would give her pleasure: she mentioned place and time at which they might conveniently encounter.

He walked with her all the way to the library, and attended her back to Gower Place. The result of this conversation was merely to intensify the conflict of feelings which Eve had excited in him. Her friendliness gave him no genuine satisfaction; her animated mood, in spite of the charm to which he submitted, disturbed him with mistrust. Nothing she said sounded quite sincere, yet it was more difficult than ever to imagine that she played a part quite alien to her disposition.

No word had fallen from her which threw light upon her present circumstances, and he feared to ask any direct question. It had surprised him to learn that she subscribed to Mudie's. The book she brought away with her was a newly published novel, and in the few words they exchanged on the subject while standing at the library counter she seemed to him to exhibit a surprising acquaintance with the literature of the day. Of his own shortcomings in this respect he was but too sensible, and he began to feel himself an intellectual inferior, where every probability had prepared him for the reverse.

The next morning he went to Mudie's on his own account, and came away with volumes chosen from those which lay on the counter. He was tired of wandering about the town, and might as well pass his time in reading.

When Sunday came, he sought the appointed spot at Hampstead, and there, after an hour's waiting, met the two friends. Eve was no longer in her vivacious mood; brilliant sunshine, and the breeze upon the heath, had no power to inspirit her; she spoke in monosyllables, and behaved with unaccountable reserve. Hilliard had no choice but to converse with Patty, who was as gay and entertaining as ever. In the course of their gossip he learnt that Miss Ringrose was employed at a music-shop, kept by her uncle, where she sold the latest songs and dances, and "tried over" on a piano any unfamiliar piece which a customer might think of purchasing. It was not easy to understand how these two girls came to be so intimate, for they seemed to have very little in common. Compared with Eve Madeley, Patty was an insignificant little person; but of her moral uprightness Hilliard felt only the more assured the longer he talked with her, and this still had a favourable effect upon his estimate of Eve.

Again there passed a few days without event. But about nine o'clock on Wednesday evening, as he sat at home over a book, his landlady entered the room with a surprising announcement.

"There's a young lady wishes to see you, Sir. Miss Ringrose is the name."

Hilliard sprang up.

"Please ask her to come in."

The woman eyed him in a manner he was too excited to understand.

"She would like to speak to you at the door, Sir, if you wouldn't mind going out."

He hastened thither. The front door stood open, and a light from the passage shone on Patty's face. In the girl's look he saw at once that something was wrong.

"Oh, Mr. Hilliard—I didn't know your number—I've been to a lot of houses asking for you——"

"What is it?" he inquired, going out on to the doorstep.

"I called to see Eve, and—I don't know what it meant, but she's gone away. The landlady says she left this morning with her luggage—went away for good. And it's so strange that she hasn't let me know anything. I can't understand it. I wanted to ask if you know——"

Hilliard stared at the house opposite.

"I? I know nothing whatever about it. Come in and tell me——"

"If you wouldn't mind coming out——"

"Yes, yes. One moment; I'll get my hat."

He rejoined the girl, and they turned in the direction of Euston Square, where people were few.

"I couldn't help coming to see you, Mr. Hilliard," said Patty, whose manner indicated the gravest concern. "It has put me in such a fright. I haven't seen her since Sunday. I came to-night, as soon as I could get away from the shop, because I didn't feel easy in my mind about her."

"Why did you feel anxious? What has been going on?"

He searched her face. Patty turned away, kept silence for a moment, and at length, with one of her wonted outbursts of confidence, said nervously:

"It's something I can't explain. But as you were a friend of hers——"

A man came by, and Patty broke off.

# CHAPTER VIII

Hilliard waited for her to continue, but Patty kept her eyes down and said no more.

"Did you think," he asked, "that I was likely to be in Miss Madeley's confidence?"

"You've known her a long time, haven't you?"

This proof of reticence, or perhaps of deliberate misleading, on Eve's part astonished Hilliard. He replied evasively that he had very little acquaintance with Miss Madeley's affairs, and added:

"May she not simply have changed her lodgings?"

"Why should she go so suddenly, and without letting me know?"

"What had the landlady to say?"

"She heard her tell the cab to drive to Mudie's—the library, you know."

"Why," said Hilliard; "that meant, perhaps, that she wanted to return a book before leaving London. Is there any chance that she has gone home—to Dudley? Perhaps her father is ill, and she was sent for."

Patty admitted this possibility, but with every sign of doubt.

"The landlady said she had a letter this morning."

"Did she? Then it may have been from Dudley. But you know her so much better than I do. Of course, you mustn't tell me anything you don't feel it right to speak of; still, did it occur to you that I could be of any use?"

"No, I didn't think; I only came because I was so upset when I found her gone. I knew you lived in Gower Place somewhere, and I thought you might have seen her since Sunday."

"I have not. But surely you will hear from her very soon. You may even get a letter to-night, or to-morrow morning."

Patty gave a little spring of hopefulness.

"Yes; a letter might come by the last post to-night. I'll go home at once."

"And I will come with you," said Hilliard. "Then you can tell me whether you have any news."

They turned and walked towards the foot of Hampstead Road, whence they could go by tram-car to Patty's abode in High Street, Camden Town. Supported by the hope of finding a letter when she arrived, Miss Ringrose grew more like herself.

"You must have wondered what*ever* I meant by calling to see you, Mr. Hilliard. I went to five or six houses before I hit on the right one. I do wish now that I'd waited a little, but I'm always doing things in that way and being sorry for them directly after. Eve is my best friend, you know, and that makes me so anxious about her."

"How long have you known her?"

"Oh, ever so long—about a year."

The temptation to make another inquiry was too strong for Hilliard.

"Where has she been employed of late?"

Patty looked up at him with surprise.

"Oh, don't you know? She isn't doing anything now. The people where she was went bankrupt, and she's been out of a place for more than a month."

"Can't find another engagement?"

"She hasn't tried yet. She's taking a holiday. It isn't very nice work, adding up money all day. I'm sure it would drive me out of my senses very soon. I think she might find something better than that."

Miss Ringrose continued to talk of her friend all the way to Camden Town, but the information he gathered did not serve to advance Hilliard in his understanding of Eve's character. That she was keeping back something of grave import the girl had already confessed, and in her chatter she frequently checked herself on the verge of an indiscretion. Hilliard took for granted that the mystery had to do with the man he had seen at Earl's Court. If Eve actually disappeared, he would not scruple to extract from Patty all that she knew; but he must see first whether Eve would communicate with her friend.

In High Street Patty entered a small shop which was on the point of being closed for the night.

Hilliard waited for her a few yards away; on her return he saw at once that she was disappointed.

"There's nothing!"

"It may come in the morning. I should like to know whether you hear or not."

"Would this be out of your way?" asked Patty. "I'm generally alone in the shop from half-past one to half-past two. There's very seldom any business going on then."

"Then I will come to-morrow at that time."

"Do, please? If I haven't heard anything I shall be that nervous."

They talked to no purpose for a few minutes, and bade each other good-night.

Next day, at the hour Patty had appointed, Hilliard was again in High Street. As he approached the shop he heard from within the jingle of a piano. A survey through the closed glass door showed him Miss Ringrose playing for her own amusement. He entered, and Patty jumped up with a smile of welcome.

"It's all right! I had a letter this morning. She *has* gone to Dudley."

"Ah! I am glad to hear it. Any reason given?"

"Nothing particular," answered the girl, striking a note on the piano with her forefinger. "She thought she might as well go home for a week or two before taking another place. She has heard of something in Holborn."

"So your alarm was groundless."

"Oh—I didn't really feel alarmed, Mr. Hilliard. You mustn't think that. I often do silly things."

Patty's look and tone were far from reassuring. Evidently she had been relieved from her suspense, but no less plainly did she seek to avoid an explanation of it. Hilliard began to glance about the shop.

"My uncle," resumed Patty, turning with her wonted sprightliness to another subject, "always goes out for an hour or two in the middle of the day to play billiards. I can tell by his face when he comes back whether he's lost or won; he does so take it to heart, silly man! Do *you* play billiards?"

The other shook his head.

"I thought not. You have a serious look."

Hilliard did not relish this compliment. He imagined he had cast away his gloom; he desired to look like the men who take life with easy courage. As he gazed through the glass door into the street, a figure suddenly blocked his prospect, and a face looked in. Then the door opened, and there entered a young man of clerkly appearance, who glanced from Miss Ringrose to her companion with an air of severity. Patty had reddened a little.

"What are *you* doing here at this time of day?" she asked familiarly.

"Oh—business—had to look up a man over here. Thought I'd speak a word as I passed."

Hilliard drew aside.

"Who has opened this new shop opposite?" added the young man, beckoning from the doorway.

A more transparent pretext for drawing Patty away could not have been conceived; but she readily lent herself to it, and followed. The door closed behind them. In a few minutes Patty returned alone, with rosy cheeks and mutinous lips.

"I'm very sorry to have been in the way," said Hilliard, smiling.

"Oh, not you. It's all right. Someone I know. He can be sensible enough when he likes, but sometimes he's such a silly there's no putting up with him. Have you heard the new waltz—the Ballroom Queen?"

She sat down and rattled over this exhilarating masterpiece.

"Thank you," said Hilliard. "You play very cleverly."

"Oh, so can anybody—that's nothing."

"Does Miss Madeley play at all?"

"No. She's always saying she wishes she could; but I tell her, what does it matter? She knows no end of things that I don't, and I'd a good deal rather have that."

"She reads a good deal, I suppose?"

"Oh, I should think she does, just! And she can speak French."

"Indeed? How did she learn?"

"At the place where she was bookkeeper there was a young lady from Paris, and they shared lodgings, and Eve learnt it from her. Then her friend went to Paris again, and Eve wanted very much to go with her, but she didn't see how to manage it. Eve," she added, with a laugh, "is always wanting to do something that's impossible."

A week later, Hilliard again called at the music-shop, and talked for half an hour with Miss Ringrose, who had no fresh news from Eve. His visits were repeated at intervals of a few days, and at length, towards the end of June, he learnt that Miss Madeley was about to return to London; she had obtained a new engagement, at the establishment in Holborn of which Patty had spoken.

"And will she come back to her old lodgings?" he inquired.

Patty shook her head.

"She'll stay with me. I wanted her to come here before, but she didn't care about it. Now she's altered her mind, and I'm very glad."

Hilliard hesitated in putting the next question.

"Do you still feel anxious about her?"

The girl met his eyes for an instant.

"No. It's all right now."

"There's one thing I should like you to tell me—if you can."

"About Miss Madeley?"

"I don't think there can be any harm in your saying yes or no. Is she engaged to be married?"

Patty replied with a certain eagerness.

"No! Indeed she isn't. And she never has been."

"Thank you." Hilliard gave a sigh of relief. "I'm very glad to know that."

"Of course you are," Patty answered, with a laugh.

As usual, after one of her frank remarks, she turned away and struck chords on the piano. Hilliard meditated the while, until his companion spoke again.

"You'll see her before long, I dare say?"

"Perhaps. I don't know."

"At all events, you'll *want* to see her."

"Most likely."

"Will you promise me something?"

"If it's in my power to keep the promise."

"It's only—I should be so glad if you wouldn't mention anything about my coming to see you that night in Gower Place."

"I won't speak of it."

"Quite sure?"

"You may depend upon me. Would you rather she didn't know that I have seen you at all?"

"Oh, there's no harm in that. I should be sure to let it out. I shall say we met by chance somewhere."

"Very well. I feel tempted to ask a promise in return."

Patty stood with her hands behind her, eyes wide and lips slightly apart.

"It is this," he continued, lowering his voice. "If ever you should begin to feel anxious again about her will you let me know?"

Her reply was delayed; it came at length in the form of an embarrassed nod. Thereupon Hilliard pressed her hand and departed.

He knew the day on which Eve would arrive in London; from

morning to night a feverish unrest drove him about the streets. On the
morrow he was scarcely more at ease, and for several days he lived
totally without occupation, save in his harassing thoughts. He paced
and repaced the length of Holborn, wondering where it was that Eve
had found employment; but from Camden Town he held aloof.

One morning there arrived for him a post-card on which was scrib-
bled: "We are going to the Savoy on Saturday night. Gallery." No
signature, no address; but of course the writer must be Patty Ringrose.
Mentally, he thanked her with much fervour. And on the stated evening, nearly an hour before the opening of the doors, he climbed the
stone steps leading to the gallery entrance of the Savoy Theatre. At the
summit two or three persons were already waiting—strangers to him.
He leaned against the wall, and read an evening paper. At every
sound of approaching feet his eyes watched with covert eagerness.
Presently he heard a laugh, echoing from below, and recognised
Patty's voice; then Miss Ringrose appeared round the winding in the
staircase, and was followed by Eve Madeley. Patty glanced up, and
smiled consciously as she discovered the face she had expected to see;
but Eve remained for some minutes unaware of her acquaintance's
proximity. Scrutinising her appearance, as he could at his ease,
Hilliard thought she looked far from well: she had a tired, dispirited
expression, and paid no heed to the people about her. Her dress was
much plainer than that she wore a month ago.

He saw Patty whispering to her companion, and, as a result, Eve's
eyes turned in his direction. He met her look, and had no difficulty in
making his way down two or three steps, to join her. The reception
she gave him was one of civil indifference. Hilliard made no remark
on what seemed the chance of their encounter, nor did he speak of her
absence from London; they talked, as far as talk was possible under
the circumstances, of theatrical and kindred subjects. He could not
perceive that the girl was either glad or sorry to have met him again;
but by degrees her mood brightened a little, and she exclaimed with
pleasure when the opening of the door caused an upward movement.

"You have been away," he said, when they were in their places, he
at one side of Eve, Patty on the other.

"Yes. At Dudley."

"Did you see Mrs. Brewer?"

"Several times. She hasn't got another lodger yet, and wishes you
would go back again. A most excellent character she gave you."

This sounded satirical.

"I deserved the best she could say of me," Hilliard answered.

Eve glanced at him, smiled doubtfully, and turned to talk with
Patty Ringrose. Through the evening there was no further mention of

Dudley. Eve could with difficulty be induced to converse at all, and when the entertainment was over she pointedly took leave of him within the theatre. But while shaking hands with Patty, he saw something in that young lady's face which caused him to nod and smile.

## CHAPTER IX

There came an afternoon early in July when Hilliard, tired with a long ramble in search of old City churches—his architectural interests never failed—sought rest and coolness in a Fleet Street tavern of time-honoured name. It was long since he had yielded to any extravagance; to-day his palate demanded wine, and with wine he solaced it. When he went forth again into the roaring highway things glowed before him in a mellow light: the sounds of Fleet Street made music to his ears; he looked with joyous benignity into the faces of men and women, and nowhere discovered a countenance inharmonious with his gallant mood.

No longer weary, he strolled westward, content with the satisfactions of each passing moment. "This," he said to himself, "is the joy of life. Past and future are alike powerless over me; I live in the glorious sunlight of this summer day, under the benediction of a great-hearted wine. Noble wine! Friend of the friendless, companion of the solitary, lifter-up of hearts that are oppressed, inspirer of brave thoughts in them that fail beneath the burden of being. Thanks to thee, O priceless wine!"

A bookseller's window arrested him. There, open to the gaze of every pedestrian, stood a volume of which the sight made him thrill with rapture; a finely illustrated folio, a treatise on the Cathedrals of France. Five guineas was the price it bore. A moment's lingering, restrained by some ignoble spirit of thrift which the wine had not utterly overcome, and he entered the shop. He purchased the volume. It would have pleased him to carry it away, but in mere good-nature he allowed the shopman's suggestion to prevail, and gave his address that the great tome might be sent to him.

How cheap it was—five guineas for so much instant delight and such boundless joy of anticipation!

On one of the benches in Trafalgar Square he sat for a long time watching the fountains, and ever and anon letting them lead his eyes upwards to the great snowy clouds that gleamed upon the profound blue. Some ragged children were at play near him; he searched his

pocket, collected coppers and small silver, and with a friendly cry of
"Holloa, you ragamuffins!" scattered amazement and delight.

St. Martin's Church told him that the hour was turned of six. Then
a purpose that had hung vaguely in his mind like a golden mist took
form and substance. He set off to walk northward, came out into
Holborn, and loitered in the neighbourhood of a certain place of business, which of late he had many times observed. It was not long that
he had to wait. Presently there came forth someone whom he knew,
and with quick steps he gained her side.

Eve Madeley perceived him without surprise.

"Yes," he said, "I am here again. If it's disagreeable to you, tell
me, and I will go my own way at once."

"I have no wish to send you away," she answered, with a smile of
self-possession. "But all the same, I think it would be wiser if you did
go."

"Ah, then, if you leave me to judge for myself——! You look tired
this evening. I have something to say to you; let us turn for a moment
up this byway."

"No, let us walk straight on."

"I beg of you!—Now you are kind. I am going to dine at a restaurant. Usually, I eat my dinner at home—a bad dinner and a cheer-
less room. On such an evening as this I can't go back and appease
hunger in that animal way. But when I sit down in the restaurant I
shall be alone. It's miserable to see the groups of people enjoying
themselves all round and to sit lonely. I can't tell you how long it is
since I had a meal in company. Will you come and dine with me?"

"I can't do that."

"Where's the impossibility?"

"I shouldn't like to do it."

"But would it be so very disagreeable to sit and talk? Or, I won't
ask you to talk; only to let me talk to you. Give me an hour or two of
your time—that's what I ask. It means so much to me, and to you,
what does it matter?"

Eve walked on in silence; his entreaties kept pace with her. At
length she stopped.

"It's all the same to me—if you wish it——"

"Thank you a thousand times!"

They walked back into Holborn, and Hilliard, talking merely of
trifles, led the way to a great hall, where some scores of people were
already dining. He selected a nook which gave assurance of privacy,
sketched to the waiter a modest but carefully chosen repast, and from
his seat on the opposite side of the table laughed silently at Eve as she
leaned back on the plush cushions. In no way disconcerted by the

show of luxury about her, Eve seemed to be reflecting, not without enjoyment.

"You would rather be here than going home in the Camden Town 'bus?"

"Of course."

"That's what I like in you. You have courage to tell the truth. When you said that you couldn't come, it was what you really thought. Now that you have learnt your mistake, you confess it."

"I couldn't have done it if I hadn't made up my mind that it was all the same, whether I came or refused."

"All the same to you. Yes; I'm quite willing that you should think it so. It puts me at my ease. I have nothing to reproach myself with. Ah, but how good it is to sit here and talk!"

"Don't you know anyone else who would come with you? Haven't you made any friends?"

"Not one. You and Miss Ringrose are the only persons I know in London."

"I can't understand why you live in that way."

"How should I make friends—among men? Why, it's harder than making money—which I have never done yet, and never shall, I'm afraid."

Eve averted her eyes, and again seemed to meditate.

"I'll tell you," pursued the young man, "how the money came to me that I am living on now. It'll fill up the few moments while we are waiting."

He made of it an entertaining narrative, which he concluded just as the soup was laid before them. Eve listened with frank curiosity, with an amused smile. Then came a lull in the conversation. Hilliard began his dinner with appetite and gusto; the girl, after a few sips, neglected her soup and glanced about the neighboring tables.

"In my position," said Hilliard at length, "what would you have done?"

"It's a difficult thing to put myself in your position."

"Is it, really? Why, then, I will tell you something more of myself. You say that Mrs. Brewer gave me an excellent character?"

"I certainly shouldn't have known you from her description."

Hilliard laughed.

"I seem to you so disreputable?"

"Not exactly that," replied Eve thoughtfully. "But you seem altogether a different person from what you seemed to her."

"Yes, I can understand that. And it gives me an opportunity for saying that you, Miss Madeley, are as different as possible from the idea I formed of you when I heard Mrs. Brewer's description."

"She described me? I should so like to hear what she said."

The changing of plates imposed a brief silence. Hilliard drank a glass of wine and saw that Eve just touched hers with her lips.

"You shall hear that—but not now. I want to enable you to judge me, and if I let you know the facts while dinner goes on it won't be so tiresome as if I began solemnly to tell you my life, as people do in novels."

He erred, if anything, on the side of brevity, but in the succeeding quarter of an hour Eve was able to gather from his careless talk, which sedulously avoided the pathetic note, a fair notion of what his existence had been from boyhood upward. It supplemented the account of himself she had received from him when they met for the first time. As he proceeded she grew more attentive, and occasionally allowed her eyes to encounter his.

"There's only one other person who has heard all this from me," he said at length. "That's a friend of mine at Birmingham—a man called Narramore. When I got Dengate's money I went to Narramore, and I told him what use I was going to make of it."

"That's what you haven't told me," remarked the listener.

"I will, now that you can understand me. I resolved to go right away from all the sights and sounds that I hated, and to live a man's life, for just as long as the money would last."

"What do you mean by a man's life?"

"Why, a life of enjoyment, instead of a life not worthy to be called life at all. This is part of it, this evening. I have had enjoyable hours since I left Dudley, but never yet one like this. And because I owe it to you, I shall remember you with gratitude as long as I remember anything at all."

"That's a mistake," said Eve. "You owe the enjoyment, whatever it is, to your money, not to me."

"You prefer to look at it in that way. Be it so. I had a delightful month in Paris, but I was driven back to England by loneliness. Now, if *you* had been there! If I could have seen you each evening for an hour or two, had dinner with you at the restaurant, talked with you about what I had seen in the day—but that would have been perfection, and I have never hoped for more than moderate, average pleasure—such as ordinary well-to-do men take as their right."

"What did you do in Paris?"

"Saw things I have longed to see any time the last fifteen years or so. Learned to talk a little French. Got to feel a better educated man than I was before."

"Didn't Dudley seem a long way off when you were there?" asked Eve half absently.

"In another planet.—You thought once of going to Paris; Miss Ringrose told me."

Eve knitted her brows, and made no answer.

## CHAPTER X

When fruit had been set before them—and as he was peeling a banana:

"What a vast difference," said Hilliard, "between the life of people who dine, and of those who don't! It isn't the mere pleasure of eating, the quality of the food—though that must have a great influence on mind and character. But to sit for an hour or two each evening in quiet, orderly enjoyment, with graceful things about one, talking of whatever is pleasant—how it civilises! Until three months ago I never dined in my life, and I know well what a change it has made in me."

"I never dined till this evening," said Eve.

"Never? This is the first time you have been at a restaurant?"

"For dinner—yes."

Hilliard heard the avowal with surprise and delight. After all, there could not have been much intimacy between her and the man she met at the Exhibition.

"When I go back to slavery," he continued, "I shall bear it more philosophically. It was making me a brute, but I think there'll be no more danger of that. The memory of civilisation will abide with me. I shall remind myself that I was once a free man, and that will support me."

Eve regarded him with curiosity.

"Is there no choice?" she asked. "While you have money, couldn't you find some better way of earning a living?"

"I have given it a thought now and then, but it's very doubtful. There's only one thing at which I might have done well, and that's architecture. From studying it just for my own pleasure, I believe I know more about architecture than most men who are not in the profession; but it would take a long time before I could earn money by it. I could prepare myself to be an architectural draughtsman, no doubt, and might do as well that way as drawing machinery. But——"

"Then why don't you go to work! It would save you from living in hideous places."

"After all, does it matter much? If I had anything else to gain. Suppose I had any hope of marriage, for instance——"

He said it playfully. Eve turned her eyes away, but gave no other sign of self-consciousness.

"I have no such hope. I have seen too much of marriage in poverty."

"So have I," said his companion, with quiet emphasis.

"And when a man's absolutely sure that he will never have an income of more than a hundred and fifty pounds——"

"It's a crime if he asks a woman to share it," Eve added coldly.

"I agree with you. It's well to understand each other on that point.—Talking of architecture, I bought a grand book this afternoon."

He described the purchase, and mentioned what it cost.

"But at that rate," said Eve, "your days of slavery will come again very soon."

"Oh! it's so rarely that I spend a large sum. On most days I satisfy myself with the feeling of freedom, and live as poorly as ever I did. Still, don't suppose that I am bent on making my money last a very long time. I can imagine myself spending it all in a week or two, and feeling I had its worth. The only question is, how can I get most enjoyment? The very best of a lifetime may come within a single day. Indeed, I believe it very often does."

"I doubt that—at least, I know that it couldn't be so with me."

"Well, what do you aim at?" Hilliard asked disinterestedly.

"Safety," was the prompt reply.

"Safety? From what?"

"From years of struggle to keep myself alive, and a miserable old age."

"Then you might have said—a safety-match."

The jest, and its unexpectedness, struck sudden laughter from Eve. Hilliard joined in her mirth.

After that she suggested, "Hadn't we better go?"

"Yes. Let us walk quietly on. The streets are pleasant after sunset."

On rising, after he had paid the bill, Hilliard chanced to see himself in a mirror. He had flushed cheeks, and his hair was somewhat disorderly. In contrast with Eve's colourless composure, his appearance was decidedly bacchanalian; but the thought merely amused him.

They crossed Holborn, and took their way up Southampton Row, neither speaking until they were within sight of Russell Square.

"I like this part of London," said Hilliard at length, pointing before him. "I often walk about the squares late at night. It's quiet, and the trees make the air taste fresh."

"I did the same, sometimes, when I lived in Gower Place."

"Doesn't it strike you that we are rather like each other in some things?"

"Oh, yes!" Eve replied frankly. "I have noticed that."

"You have? Even in the lives we have led there's a sort of resemblance, isn't there?"

"Yes, I see now that there is."

In Russell Square they turned from the pavement, and walked along the edge of the enclosure.

"I wish Patty had been with us," said Eve all at once. "She would have enjoyed it so thoroughly."

"To be sure she would. Well, we can dine again, and have Patty with us. But, after all, dining in London can't be quite what it is in Paris. I wish you hadn't gone back to work again. Do you know what I should have proposed?"

She glanced inquiringly at him.

"Why shouldn't we all have gone to Paris for a holiday? You and Patty could have lived together, and I should have seen you every day."

Eve laughed.

"Why not? Patty and I have both so much more money than we know what to do with," she answered.

"Money? Oh, what of that! I have money."

She laughed again.

Hilliard was startled.

"You are talking rather wildly. Leaving myself out of the question, what would Mr. Dally say to such a proposal?"

"Who's Mr. Dally?"

"Don't you know? Hasn't Patty told you that she is engaged?"

"Ah! No; she hasn't spoken of it. But I think I must have seen him at the music-shop one day. Is she likely to marry him?"

"It isn't the wisest thing she could do, but that may be the end of it. He's in an auctioneer's office, and may have a pretty good income some day."

A long silence followed. They passed out of Russell into Woburn Square. Night was now darkening the latest tints of the sky, and the lamps shone golden against dusty green. At one of the houses in the narrow square festivities were toward; carriages drew up before the entrance, from which a red carpet was laid down across the pavement; within sounded music.

"Does this kind of thing excite any ambition in you?" Hilliard asked, coming to a pause a few yards away from the carriage which was discharging its occupants.

"Yes, I suppose it does. At all events, it makes me feel discontented."

"I have settled all that with myself. I am content to look on as if it were a play. Those people have an idea of life quite different from mine. I shouldn't enjoy myself among them. You, perhaps, would."

"I might," Eve replied absently. And she turned away to the other side of the square.

"By-the-bye, you *have* a friend in Paris. Do you ever hear from her?"

"She wrote once or twice after she went back; but it has come to an end."

"Still, you might find her again, if you were there."

Eve delayed her reply a little, then spoke impatiently.

"What is the use of setting my thoughts upon such things? Day after day I try to forget what I most wish for. Talk about yourself, and I will listen with pleasure; but never talk about me."

"It's very hard to lay that rule upon me. I want to hear you speak of yourself. As yet, I hardly know you, and I never shall unless you——"

"Why should you know me?" she interrupted, in a voice of irritation.

"Only because I wish it more than anything else. I have wished it from the day when I first saw your portrait."

"Oh! that wretched portrait! I should be sorry if I thought it was at all like me."

"It is both like and unlike," said Hilliard. "What I see of it in your face is the part of you that most pleases me."

"And that isn't my real self at all."

"Perhaps not. And yet, perhaps, you are mistaken. That is what I want to learn. From the portrait, I formed an idea of you. When I met you, it seemed to me that I was hopelessly astray; yet now I don't feel sure of it."

"You would like to know what has changed me from the kind of girl I was at Dudley?"

"*Are* you changed?"

"In some ways, no doubt. You, at all events, seem to think so."

"I can wait. You will tell me all about it some day."

"You mustn't take that for granted. We have made friends in a sort of way, just because we happened to come from the same place, and know the same people. But——"

He waited.

"Well, I was going to say that there's no use in our thinking much about each other."

"I don't ask you to think of me. But I shall think a great deal about you for long enough to come."

"That's what I want to prevent."

"Why?"

"Because, in the end, it might be troublesome to me."

Hilliard kept silence awhile, then laughed. When he spoke again, it was of things indifferent.

# CHAPTER XI

Laziest of men and worst of correspondents, Robert Narramore had as yet sent no reply to the letters in which Hilliard acquainted him with his adventures in London and abroad; but at the end of July he vouchsafed a perfunctory scrawl. "Too bad not to write before, but I've been floored every evening after business in this furious heat. You may like to hear that my uncle's property didn't make a bad show. I have come in for a round five thousand, and am putting it into brass bedsteads. Sha'n't be able to get away until the end of August. May see you then." Hilliard mused enviously on the brass bedstead business.

On looking in at the Camden Town music-shop about this time he found Patty Ringrose flurried and vexed by an event which disturbed her prospects. Her uncle the shopkeeper, a widower of about fifty, had announced his intention of marrying again, and, worse still, of giving up his business.

"It's the landlady of the public-house where he goes to play billiards," said Patty with scornful mirth; "a great fat woman! Oh! And he's going to turn publican. And my aunt and me will have to look out for ourselves."

This aunt was the shopkeeper's maiden sister who had hitherto kept house for him. "She had been promised an allowance," said Patty, "but a very mean one."

"I don't care much for myself," the girl went on; "there's plenty of shops where I can get an engagement, but of course it won't be the same as here, which has been home for me ever since I was a child. There! the things that men will do! I've told him plain to his face that he ought to be ashamed of himself, and so has aunt. And he *is* ashamed, what's more. Don't you call it disgusting, such a marriage as that?"

Hilliard avoided the delicate question.

"I shouldn't wonder if it hastens another marriage," he said with a smile.

"I know what you mean, but the chances are that marriage won't come off at all. I'm getting tired of men; they're so selfish and unreasonable. Of course I don't mean you, Mr. Hilliard, but—oh! you know what I mean."

"Mr. Dally has fallen under your displeasure?"

"Please don't talk about him. If he thinks he's going to lay down the law to me he'll find his mistake; and it's better he should find it out before it's too late."

They were interrupted by the entrance of Patty's amorous uncle, who returned from his billiards earlier than usual to-day. He scowled at the stranger, but passed into the house without speaking. Hilliard spoke a hurried word or two about Eve and went his way.

Something less than a week after this he chanced to be away from home throughout the whole day, and on returning he was surprised to see a telegram upon his table. It came from Patty Ringrose, and asked him to call at the shop without fail between one and two that day. The hour was now nearly ten; the despatch had arrived at eleven in the morning.

Without a minute's delay he ran out in search of a cab, and was driven to High Street. Here, of course, he found the shop closed, but it was much too early for the household to have retired to rest; risking an indiscretion, he was about to ring the house bell when the door opened, and Patty showed herself.

"Oh, is it *you*, Mr. Hilliard!" she exclaimed, in a flurried voice. "I heard the cab stop, and I thought it might be—— You'd better come in—quick!"

He followed her along the passage and into the shop, where one gas-jet was burning low.

"Listen!" she resumed, whispering hurriedly. "If Eve comes— she'll let herself in with the latchkey—you must stand quiet here. I shall turn out the gas, and I'll let you out after she's gone upstairs. Couldn't you come before?"

Hilliard explained, and begged her to tell him what was the matter. But Patty kept him in suspense.

"Uncle won't be in till after twelve, so there's no fear. Aunt has gone to bed—she's upset with quarrelling about this marriage. Mind! You won't stir if Eve comes in. Don't talk loud; I must keep listening for the door."

"But what is it? Where is Eve?"

"I don't know. She didn't come home till very late last night, and I don't know where she was. You remember what you asked me to promise?"

"To let me know if you were anxious about her."

"Yes, and I am. She's in danger. I only hope——"

"What?"

"I don't like to tell you all I know. It doesn't seem right. But I'm so afraid for Eve."

"I can only imagine one kind of danger——"

"Yes—of course, it's that—you know what I mean. But there's more than you could fancy."

"Tell me, then, what has alarmed you?"

"When did you see her last?" Patty inquired.

"More than a week ago. Two or three days before I came here."

"Had you noticed anything?"

"Nothing unusual."

"No more did I, till last Monday night. Then I saw that something was wrong. Hush!"

She gripped his arm, and they listened. But no sound could be heard.

"And since then," Patty pursued, with tremulous eagerness, "she's been very queer. I know she doesn't sleep at night, and she's getting ill, and she's had letters from—someone she oughtn't to have anything to do with."

"Having told so much, you had better tell me all," said Hilliard impatiently. There was a cold sweat on his forehead, and his heart beat painfully.

"No. I can't. I can only give you a warning."

"But what's the use of that? What can I do? How can I interfere?"

"I don't know," replied the girl, with a helpless sigh. "She's in danger, that's all I can tell you."

"Patty, don't be a fool! Out with it! Who is the man? Is it someone you know?"

"I don't exactly know him. I've seen him."

"Is he—a sort of gentleman?"

"Oh, yes, he's a gentleman. And you'd never think to look at him that he could do anything that wasn't right."

"Very well. What reason have you for supposing that he's doing wrong?"

Patty kept silence. A band of rowdy fellows just then came shouting along the street, and one of them crashed up against the shop door, making Patty jump and scream. Oaths and foul language followed; and then the uproar passed away.

"Look here," said Hilliard. "You'll drive me out of my senses. Eve is in love with this man, is she?"

"I'm afraid so. She was."

"Before she went away, you mean. And, of course, her going away had something to do with it?"

"Yes, it had."

Hilliard laid his hands on the girl's shoulders.

"You've got to tell me the plain truth, and be quick about it. I suppose you haven't any idea of the torments I'm suffering. I shall begin to think you're making a fool of me, and that there's nothing but— though that's bad enough for me."

"Very well, I'll tell you. She went away because it came out that the man was married."

"Oh, that's it?" He spoke from a dry throat. "She told you herself?"

"Yes, not long after she came back. She said, of course, she could have no more to do with him. She used to meet him pretty often——"

"Stay, how did she get to know him first?"

"Just by chance—somewhere."

"I understand," said Hilliard grimly. "Go on."

"And his wife got someone to spy on him, and they found out he was meeting Eve, and she jumped out on them when they were walking somewhere together, and told Eve everything. He wasn't living with his wife, and hasn't been for a long time."

"What's his position?"

"He's in business, and seems to have lots of money; but I don't exactly know what it is he does."

"You are afraid, then, that Eve is being drawn back to him?"

"I feel sure she is—and it's dreadful."

"What I should like to know," said Hilliard, harshly, "is whether she really cares for him, or only for his money."

"Oh! How horrid you are! I never thought you could say such a thing!"

"Perhaps you didn't. All the same, it's a question. I don't pretend to understand Eve Madeley, and I'm afraid you are just as far from knowing her."

"I don't know her? Why, what are you talking about, Mr. Hilliard?"

"What do you think of her, then? Is she a good-hearted girl or——"

"Or what? Of course she's good-hearted. The things that men do say! They seem to be all alike."

"Women are so far from being all alike that one may think she understands another, and be utterly deceived. Eve has shown her best side to you, no doubt. With me, she hasn't taken any trouble to do so. And if——"

"Hush!"

This time the alarm was justified. A latchkey rattled at the house-door, the door opened, and in the same moment Patty turned out the light.

"It's my uncle," she whispered, terror-stricken. "Don't stir."

# CHAPTER XII

A heavy footstep sounded in the passage, and Hilliard, to whose emotions was now added a sense of ludicrous indignity, heard talk between Patty and her uncle.

"You mustn't lock up yet," said the girl, "Eve is out."

"What's she doing?"

"I don't know. At the theatre with friends, I dare say."

"If we'd been staying on here, that young woman would have had to look out for another lodging. There's something I don't like about her, and if you take my advice, Patty, you'll shake her off. She'll do you no good, my girl."

They passed together into the room behind the shop, and though their voices were still audible, Hilliard could no longer follow the conversation. He stood motionless, just where Patty had left him, with a hand resting on the top of the piano, and it seemed to him that at least half an hour went by. Then a sound close by made him start; it was the snapping of a violin string; the note reverberated through the silent shop. But by this time the murmur of conversation had ceased, and Hilliard hoped that Patty's uncle had gone upstairs to bed.

As proved to be the case. Presently the door opened, and a voice called to him in a whisper. He obeyed the summons, and, not without stumbling, followed Patty into the open air.

"She hasn't come yet."

"What's the time?"

"Half-past eleven. I shall sit up for her. Did you hear what my uncle said? You mustn't think anything of that; he's always finding fault with people."

"Do you think she will come at all?" asked Hilliard.

"Oh, of course she will!"

"I shall wait about. Don't stand here. Good-night."

"You won't let her know what I've told you?" said Patty, retaining his hand.

"No, I won't. If she doesn't come back at all, I'll see you to-morrow."

He moved away, and the door closed.

Many people were still passing along the street. In his uncertainty as to the direction by which Eve would return—if return she did—Hilliard ventured only a few yards away. He had waited for about a quarter of an hour, when his eye distinguished a well-known figure quickly approaching. He hurried forward, and Eve stopped before he had quite come up to her.

"Where have you been to-night?" were his first words, sounding more roughly than he intended.

"I wanted to see you. I passed your lodgings and saw there was no light in the windows, else I should have asked for you."

She spoke in so strange a voice, with such show of agitation, that Hilliard stood gazing at her till she again broke silence.

"Have you been waiting here for me?"

"Yes. Patty told me you weren't back."

"Why did you come?"

"Why do I ever come to meet you?"

"We can't talk here," said Eve, turning away. "Come into a quieter place."

They walked in silence to the foot of High Street, and there turned aside into the shadowed solitude of Mornington Crescent. Eve checked her steps and said abruptly——

"I want to ask you for something."

"What is it?"

"Now that it comes to saying it, I—I'm afraid. And yet if I had asked you that evening when we were at the restaurant——"

"What is it?" Hilliard repeated gruffly.

"That isn't your usual way of speaking to me."

"Will you tell me where you have been to-night?"

"Nowhere—walking about——"

"Do you often walk about the streets till midnight?"

"Indeed I don't."

The reply surprised him by its humility. Her voice all but broke on the words. As well as the dim light would allow, he searched her face, and it seemed to him that her eyes had a redness, as if from shedding tears.

"You haven't been alone?"

"No—I've been with a friend."

"Well, I have no claim upon you. It's nothing to me what friends you go about with. What were you going to ask of me?"

"You have changed so all at once. I thought you would never talk in this way."

"I didn't mean to," said Hilliard. "I have lost control of myself, that's all. But you can say whatever you meant to say—just as you would have done at the restaurant. I'm the same man I was then."

Eve moved a few steps, but he did not follow her, and she returned. A policeman passing threw a glance at them.

"It's no use asking what I meant to ask," she said, with her eyes on the ground. "You won't grant it me."

"How can I say till I know what it is? There are not many things in my power that I wouldn't do for you."

"I was going to ask for money."

"Money? Why, it depends what you are going to do with it. If it will do you any good, all the money I have is yours, as you know well enough. But I must understand why you want it."

"I can't tell you that. I don't want you to give me money—only to lend it. You shall have it back again, though I can't promise the exact time. If you hadn't changed so, I should have found it easy enough to ask. But I don't know you to-night; it's like talking to a stranger. What has happened to make you so different?"

"I have been waiting a long time for you, that's all," Hilliard replied, endeavouring to use the tone of frank friendliness in which he had been wont to address her. "I got nervous and irritable. I felt uneasy about you. It's all right now. Let us walk on a little. You want money. Well, I have three hundred pounds and more. Call it mine, call it yours. But I must know that you're not going to do anything foolish. Of course, you don't tell me everything; I have no right to expect it. You haven't misled me; I knew from the first that—well, a girl of your age, and with your face, doesn't live alone in London without adventures. I shouldn't think of telling you all mine, and I don't ask to know yours—unless I begin to have a part in them. There's something wrong: of course, I can see that. I think you've been crying, and you don't shed tears for a trifle. Now you come and ask me for money. If it will do you good, take all you want. But I've an uncomfortable suspicion that harm may come of it."

"Why not treat me just like a man-friend? I'm old enough to take care of myself."

"You think so, but I know better. Wait a moment. How much money do you want?"

"Thirty-five pounds."

"Exactly thirty-five? And it isn't for your own use?"

"I can't tell you any more. I am in very great need of the money, and if you will lend it me I shall feel very grateful."

"I want no gratitude, I want nothing from you, Eve, except what you can't give me. I can imagine a man in my position giving you money in the hope that it might be your ruin; just to see you brought down, humiliated. There's so much of the brute in us all. But I don't feel that desire."

"Why should you?" she asked, with a change to coldness. "What harm have I done you?"

"No harm at all, and perhaps a great deal of good. I say that I wish you nothing but well. Suppose a gift of all the money I have would smooth your whole life before you, and make you the happy wife of some other man. I would give it you gladly. That kind of thing has often been said, when it meant nothing: it isn't so with me. It has

always been more pleasure to me to give than to receive. No merit of
mine; I have it from my father. Make clear to me that you are to
benefit by this money, and you shall have the cheque as soon as you
please."

"I shall benefit by it, because it will relieve me from a dreadful
anxiety."

"Or, in other words, will relieve someone else?"

"I can speak only of myself. The kindness will be done to me."

"I must know more than that. Come now, we assume that there's
someone in the background. A friend of yours, let us say. I can't
imagine why this friend of yours wants money, but so it is. You don't
contradict me?"

Eve remained mute, her head bent.

"What about your friend and you in the future? Are you bound to
this friend in any irredeemable way?"

"No—I am not," she answered, with emotion.

"There's nothing between you but—let us call it mere friendship."

"Nothing—nothing!"

"So far, so good." He looked keenly into her face. "But how about
the future?"

"There will never be anything more—there can't be."

"Let us say that you think so at present. Perhaps I don't feel quite
so sure of it. I say again, it's nothing to me, unless I get drawn into it
by you yourself. I am not your guardian. If I tell you to be careful, it's
an impertinence. But the money; that's another affair. I won't help
you to misery."

"You will be helping me *out* of misery!" Eve exclaimed.

"Yes, for the present. I will make a bargain with you."

She looked at him with startled eyes.

"You shall have your thirty-five pounds on condition that you go to
live, for as long as I choose, in Paris. You are to leave London in a
day or two. Patty shall go with you; her uncle doesn't want her, and
she seems to have quarrelled with the man she was engaged to. The
expenses are my affair. I shall go to Paris myself, and be there while
you are, but you need see no more of me than you like. Those are the
terms."

"I can't think you are serious," said Eve.

"Then I'll explain why I wish you to do this. I've thought about
you a great deal; in fact, since we first met, my chief occupation has
been thinking about you. And I have come to the conclusion that you
are suffering from an illness, the result of years of hardship and
misery. We have agreed, you remember, that there are a good many
points of resemblance between your life and mine, and perhaps
between your character and mine. Now I myself, when I escaped from

Dudley, was thoroughly ill—body and soul. The only hope for me was a complete change of circumstances—to throw off the weight of my past life, and learn the meaning of repose, satisfaction, enjoyment. I prescribe the same for you. I am your physician; I undertake your cure. If you refuse to let me, there's an end of everything between us; I shall say good-bye to you to-night, and to-morrow set off for some foreign country."

"How can I leave my work at a moment's notice?"

"The devil take your work—for he alone is the originator of such accursed toil!"

"How can I live at your expense?"

"That's a paltry obstacle. Oh, if you are too proud, say so, and there's an end of it. You know me well enough to feel the absolute truth of what I say, when I assure you that you will remain just as independent of me as you ever were. I shall be spending my money in a way that gives me pleasure; the matter will never appear to me in any other light. Why, call it an additional loan, if it will give any satisfaction to you. You are to pay me back some time. Here in London you perish; across the Channel there, health of body and mind is awaiting you; and are we to talk about money? I shall begin to swear like a trooper; the thing is too preposterous."

Eve said nothing: she stood half turned from him.

"Of course," he pursued, "you may object to leave London. Perhaps the sacrifice is too great. In that case, I should only do right if I carried you off by main force; but I'm afraid it can't be; I must leave you to perish."

"I am quite willing to go away," said Eve in a low voice. "But the shame of it—to be supported by you."

"Why, you don't hate me?"

"You know I do not."

"You even have a certain liking for me. I amuse you; you think me an odd sort of fellow, perhaps with more good than bad in me. At all events, you can trust me?"

"I can trust you perfectly."

"And it ain't as if I wished you to go alone. Patty will be off her head with delight when the thing is proposed to her."

"But how can I explain to her?"

"Don't attempt to. Leave her curiosity a good hard nut to crack. Simply say you are off to Paris, and that if she'll go with you, you will bear all her expenses."

"It's so difficult to believe that you are in earnest."

"You must somehow bring yourself to believe it. There will be a cheque ready for you to-morrow morning, to take or refuse. If you take it, you are bound in honour to leave England not later than—

we'll say Thursday. That you are to be trusted, I believe, just as firmly as you believe it of me."

"I can't decide to-night."

"I can give you only till to-morrow morning. If I don't hear from you by midday, I am gone."

"You shall hear from me—one way or the other."

"Then don't wait here any longer. It's after midnight, and Patty will be alarmed about you. No, we won't shake hands; not that till we strike a bargain."

Eve seemed about to walk away, but she hesitated and turned again.

"I will do as you wish—I will go."

"Excellent! Then speak of it to Patty as soon as possible, and tell me what she says when we meet to-morrow—where and when you like."

"In this same place, at nine o'clock."

"So be it. I will bring the cheque."

"But I must be able to cash it at once."

"So you can. It will be on a London bank. I'll get the cash myself if you like."

Then they shook hands and went in opposite directions.

## CHAPTER XIII

On the evening of the next day, just after he had lit his lamp, Hilliard's attention was drawn by a sound as of someone tapping at the window. He stood to listen, and the sound was repeated—an unmistakable tap of fingers on the glass. In a moment he was out in the street, where he discovered Patty Ringrose.

"Why didn't you come to see me?" she asked excitedly.

"I was afraid *she* might be there. Did she go to business, as usual?"

"Yes. At least I suppose so. She only got home at the usual time. I've left her there: I was bound to see you. Do you know what she told me last night when she came in?"

"I dare say I could guess."

Hilliard began to walk down the street. Patty, keeping close at his side, regarded him with glances of wonder.

"Is it true that we're going to Paris? I couldn't make out whether she meant it, and this morning I couldn't get a word from her."

"Are you willing to go with her?"

"And have all my expenses paid?"

"Of course."

"I should think I am! But I daren't let my uncle and aunt know; there's be no end of bother. I shall have to make up some sort of tale to satisfy my aunt, and get my things sent to the station while uncle's playing billiards. How long is it for?"

"Impossible to say. Three months—half a year—I don't know. What about Mr. Dally?"

"Oh, I've done with *him!*"

"And you are perfectly sure that you can get employment whenever you need it?"

"Quite sure: no need to trouble about that. I'm very good friends with aunt, and she'll take me in for as long as I want when I come back. But it's easy enough for anybody like me to get a place. I've had two or three offers the last half-year, from good shops where they were losing their young ladies. We're always getting married, in our business, and places have to be filled up."

"That settles it, then."

"But I want to know—I can't make it out—Eve won't tell me how she's managing to go. Are *you* going to pay for her?"

"We won't talk of that, Patty. She's going; that's enough."

"You persuaded her, last night?"

"Yes, I persuaded her. And I am to hear by the first post in the morning whether she will go to-morrow or Thursday. She'll arrange things with you to-night, I should think."

"It didn't look like it. She's shut herself in her room."

"I can understand that. She is ill. That's why I'm getting her away from London. Wait till we've been in Paris a few weeks, and you'll see how she changes. At present she is downright ill—ill enough to go to bed and be nursed, if that would do any good. It's your part to look after her. I don't want you to be her servant."

"Oh, I don't mind doing anything for her."

"No, because you are a very good sort of girl. You'll live at a hotel, and what you have to do is to make her enjoy herself. I shouldn't wonder if you find it difficult at first, but we shall get her round before long."

"I never thought there was anything the matter with her."

"Perhaps not, but I understand her better. Of course you won't say a word of this to her. You take it as a holiday—as good fun. No doubt I shall be able to have a few words in private with you now and then. But at other times we must talk as if nothing special had passed between us."

Patty mused. The lightness of her step told in what a spirit of gaiety she looked forward to the expedition.

"Do you think," she asked presently, "that it'll all come to an end—what I told you of?"

"Yes, I think so."

"You didn't let her know that I'd been talking——"

"Of course not. And, as I don't want her to know that you've seen me to-night, you had better stay no longer. She's sure to have something to tell you to-night or to-morrow morning. Get your packing done, and be ready at any moment. When I hear from Eve in the morning, I shall send her a telegram. Most likely we sha'n't see each other again until we meet at Charing Cross. I hope it may be to-morrow; but Thursday is the latest."

So Patty took her departure, tripping briskly homeward. As for Hilliard, he returned to his sitting-room, and was busy for some time with the pencilling of computations in English and French money. Towards midnight, he walked as far as High Street, and looked at the windows above the music-shop. All was dark.

He rose very early next morning, and as post-time drew near he walked about the street in agonies of suspense. He watched the letter-carrier from house to house, followed him up, and saw him pass the number at which he felt assured that he would deliver a letter. In frenzy of disappointment a fierce oath burst from his lips.

"That's what comes of trusting a woman!—she is going to cheat me. She has gained her end, and will put me off with excuses."

But perhaps a telegram would come. He made a pretence of breakfasting, and paced his room for an hour like a caged animal. When the monotony of circulating movement had all but stupefied him, he was awakened by a double postman's knock at the front door, the signal that announces a telegram.

Again from Patty, and again a request that he would come to the shop at mid-day.

"Just as I foresaw—excuses—postponement. What woman ever had the sense of honour!"

To get through the morning he drank—an occupation suggested by the heat of the day, which blazed cloudless. The liquor did not cheer him, but inspired a sullen courage, a reckless resolve. And in this frame of mind he presented himself before Patty Ringrose.

"She can't go to-day," said Patty, with an air of concern. "You were quite right—she is really ill."

"Has she gone out?"

"No, she's upstairs, lying on the bed. She says she has a dreadful headache, and if you saw her you'd believe it. She looks shocking. It's the second night she hasn't closed her eyes."

A savage jealousy was burning Hilliard's vitals. He had tried to make light of the connection between Eve and that unknown man, even after her extraordinary request for money, which all but confessedly she wanted on his account. He had blurred the significance of such a situation, persuading himself that neither was Eve capable of a great passion, nor the man he had seen able to inspire one. Now he rushed to the conviction that Eve had fooled him with a falsehood.

"Tell her this." He glared at Patty with eyes which made the girl shrink in alarm. "If she isn't at Charing Cross Station by a quarter to eleven to-morrow, there's an end of it. I shall be there, and shall go on without her. It's her only chance."

"But if she really *can't*——"

"Then it's her misfortune—she must suffer for it. She goes to-morrow or not at all. Can you make her understand that?"

"I'll tell her."

"Listen, Patty. If you bring her safe to the station to-morrow you shall have a ten-pound note, to buy what you like in Paris."

The girl reddened, half in delight, half in shame.

"I don't want it—she shall come——"

"Very well; good-bye till to-morrow, or for good."

"No, no; she shall come."

He was drenched in perspiration, yet walked for a mile or two at his topmost speed. Then a consuming thirst drove him into the nearest place where drink was sold. At six o'clock he remembered that he had not eaten since breakfast; he dined extravagantly, and afterwards fell asleep in the smoking-room of the restaurant. A waiter with difficulty aroused him, and persuaded him to try the effect of the evening air. An hour later he sank in exhaustion on one of the benches near the river, and there slept profoundly until stirred by a policeman.

"What's the time?" was his inquiry, as he looked up at the starry sky.

He felt for his watch, but no watch was discoverable. Together with the gold chain it had disappeared.

"Damnation! Someone has robbed me."

The policeman was sympathetic, but reproachful.

"Why do you go to sleep on the Embankment at this time of night? Lost any money?"

Yes, his money too had flown; luckily, only a small sum. It was for the loss of his watch and chain that he grieved; they had been worn for years by his father, and on that account had a far higher value for him than was represented by their mere cost.

As a matter of form, he supplied the police with information concerning the theft. Of recovery there could be little hope.

Thoroughly awakened and sober, he walked across London to Gower Place arriving in the light of dawn. Too spiritless to take off his clothing, he lay upon the bed, and through the open window watched a great cloud that grew rosy above the opposite houses.

Would Eve be at the place of meeting to-day? It seemed to him totally indifferent whether she came or not; nay, he all but hoped that she would not. He had been guilty of prodigious folly. The girl belonged to another man; and even had it not been so, what was the use of flinging away his money at this rate? Did he look for any reward correspondent to the sacrifice? She would never love him, and it was not in his power to complete the work he had begun, by freeing her completely from harsh circumstances, setting her in a path of secure and pleasant life.

But she would not come, and so much the better. With only himself to provide for he had still money enough to travel far. He would see something of the great world, and leave his future to destiny.

He dozed for an hour or two.

Whilst he was at breakfast a letter arrived for him. He did not know the handwriting on the envelope, but it must be Eve's. Yes. She wrote a couple of lines:

> I will be at the station to-morrow at a quarter to eleven.
> ——E. M.

## CHAPTER XIV

One travelling bag was all he carried. Some purchases that he had made in London—especially the great work on French cathedrals— were already despatched to Birmingham, to lie in the care of Robert Narramore.

He reached Charing Cross half an hour before train-time, and waited at the entrance. Several cabs that drove up stirred his expectation only to disappoint him. He was again in an anguish of fear lest Eve should not come. A cab arrived, with two boxes of modest appearance. He stepped forward and saw the girls' faces.

Between him and Eve not a word passed. They avoided each other's look. Patty, excited and confused, shook hands with him.

"Go on to the platform," he said. "I'll see after everything. This is all the luggage?"

"Yes. One box is mine, and one Eve's. I had to face it out with the people at home," she added, between laughing and crying. "They think I'm going to the seaside, to stay with Eve till she gets better. I never told so many fibs in my life. Uncle stormed at me, but I don't care."

"All right; go on to the platform."

Eve was already walking in that direction. Undeniably she looked ill; her step was languid; she did not raise her eyes. Hilliard, when he had taken tickets and booked the luggage through to Paris, approached his travelling companions. Seeing him, Eve turned away.

"I shall go in a smoking compartment," he said to Patty. "You had better take your tickets."

"But when shall we see you again?"

"Oh, at Dover, of course."

"Will it be rough, do you think? I do wish Eve would talk. I can't get a word out of her. It makes it all so miserable, when we might be enjoying ourselves."

"Don't trouble: leave her to herself. I'll get you some papers."

On returning from the bookstall, he slipped loose silver into Patty's hands.

"Use that if you want anything on the journey. And—I haven't forgot my promise."

"Nonsense!"

"Go and take your places now: there's only ten minutes to wait."

He watched them as they passed the barrier. Neither of the girls was dressed very suitably for travelling; but Eve's costume resembled that of a lady, while Patty's might suggest that she was a lady's-maid. As if to confirm this distinction, Patty had burdened herself with several small articles, whereas her friend carried only a sunshade. They disappeared among people upon the platform. In a few minutes Hilliard followed, glanced along the carriages till he saw where the girls were seated, and took his own place. He wore a suit which had been new on his first arrival in London, good enough in quality and cut to give his features the full value of their intelligence; a brown felt hat, a russet necktie, a white flannel shirt. Finding himself with a talkative neighbour in the carriage, he chatted freely. As soon as the train had started, he lit his pipe and tasted the tobacco with more relish than for a long time.

On board the steamer Eve kept below from first to last. Patty walked the deck with Hilliard, and vastly to her astonishment, achieved the voyage without serious discomfort. Hilliard himself, with the sea wind in his nostrils, recovered that temper of buoyant satisfaction which had accompanied his first escape from London. He despised the weak misgivings and sordid calculations of yesterday. Here he was, on a Channel steamer, bearing away from disgrace and wretchedness the woman whom his heart desired. Wild as the project had seemed to him when first he conceived it, he had put it into execution. The moment was worth living for. Whatever the future might keep in store for him of dreary, toilsome, colourless existence, the retrospect would always show him this patch of purple—a memory precious beyond all the possible results of prudence and narrow self-regard.

The little she-Cockney by his side entertained him with the flow of her chatter; it had the advantage of making him feel a travelled man.

"I didn't cross this way when I came before," he explained to her.

"From Newhaven it's a much longer voyage."

"You like the sea, then?"

"I chose it because it was cheaper—that's all."

"Yet you're so extravagant now," remarked Patty, with eyes that confessed admiration of this quality.

"Oh, because I am rich," he answered gaily. "Money is nothing to me."

"Are you really rich? Eve said you weren't."

"Did she?"

"I don't mean she said it in a disagreeable way. It was last night. She thought you were wasting your money upon us."

"If I choose to waste it, why not? Isn't there a pleasure in doing as you like?"

"Oh, of course there is," Patty assented. "I only wish I had the chance. But it's awfully jolly, this! Who'd have thought, a week ago, that I should be going to Paris? I have a feeling all the time that I shall wake up and find I've been dreaming."

"Suppose you go down and see whether Eve wants anything? You needn't say I sent you."

From Calais to Paris he again travelled apart from the girls. Fatigue overcame him, and for the last hour or two he slept, with the result that, on alighting at the Gare du Nord, he experienced a decided failure of spirits. Happily, there was nothing before him but to carry out a plan already elaborated. With the aid of his guide-book he had selected an hotel which seemed suitable for the girls, one where English was spoken, and thither he drove with them from the station. The choice of their rooms, and the settlement of details took only a few minutes; then, for almost the first time since leaving Charing Cross, he spoke to Eve.

"Patty will do everything she can for you," he said; "I shall be not very far away, and you can always send me a message if you wish. To-morrow morning I shall come at about ten to ask how you are—nothing more than that—unless you care to go anywhere."

The only reply was "Thank you," in a weary tone. And so, having taken his leave he set forth to discover a considerably less expensive lodging for himeslf. In this, after his earlier acquaintance with Paris, he had no difficulty; by half-past eight his business was done, and he sat down to dinner at a cheap restaurant. A headache spoilt his enjoyment of the meal. After a brief ramble about the streets, he went home and got into a bed which was rather too short for him, but otherwise promised sufficient comfort.

The first thing that came into his mind when he awoke next morning was that he no longer possessed a watch; the loss cast a gloom upon him. But he had slept well, and a flood of sunshine that streamed over his scantily carpeted floor, together with gladly remembered sounds from the street, soon put him into an excellent humour. He sprang up, partly dressed himself, and unhasped the window. The smell of Paris had become associated in his mind with thoughts of liberty; a grotesque dance about the bed-room expressed his joy.

As he anticipated, Patty alone received him when he called upon the girls. She reported that Eve felt unable to rise.

"What do you think about her?" he asked. "Nothing serious, is it?"

"She can't get rid of her headache."

"Let her rest as long as she likes. Are you comfortable here?"

Patty was in ecstasies with everything, and chattered on breathlessly. She wished to go out; Eve had no need of her—indeed had told her that above all she wished to be left alone.

"Get ready, then," said Hilliard, "and we'll have an hour or two."

They walked to the Madeleine and rode thence on the top of a tram-car to the Bastille. By this time Patty had come to regard her strange companion in a sort of brotherly light; no restraint whatever appeared in her conversation with him. Eve, she told him, had talked French with the chambermaid.

"And I fancy it was something she didn't want *me* to understand."

"Why should you think so?"

"Oh, something in the way the girl looked at me."

"No, no; you were mistaken. She only wanted to show that she knew some French."

But Hilliard wondered whether Patty could be right. Was it not possible that Eve had gratified her vanity by representing her friend as a servant—a lady's-maid? Yet why should he attribute such a fault to her? It was an odd thing that he constantly regarded Eve in the least favourable light, giving weight to all the ill he conjectured in her, and minimising those features of her character which, at the beginning, he had been prepared to observe with sympathy and admiration. For a man in love his reflections followed a very unwonted course. And, indeed, he had never regarded his love as of very high or pure quality; it was something that possessed him and constrained him—by no means a source of elevating emotion.

"Do you like Eve?" he asked abruptly, disregarding some trivial question Patty had put to him.

"Like her? Of course I do."

"And *why* do you like her?"

"Why?—ah—I don't know. Because I do."

And she laughed foolishly.

"Does Eve like *you?*" Hilliard continued.

"I think she does. Else I don't see why she kept up with me."

"Has she ever done you any kindness?"

"I'm sure I don't know. Nothing particular. She never gave anything, if you mean that. But she has paid for me at theatres and so on."

Hilliard quitted the subject.

"If you like to go out alone," he told her before they parted, "there's no reason why you shouldn't—just as you do in London. Remember the way back, that's all, and don't be out late. And you'll want some French money."

"But I don't understand it, and how can I buy anything when I can't speak a word?"

"All the same, take that and keep it till you are able to make use of it. It's what I promised you."

Patty drew back her hand, but her objections were not difficult to overcome.

"I dare say," Hilliard continued, "Eve doesn't understand the money much better than you do. But she'll soon be well enough to talk, and then I shall explain everything to her. On this piece of paper is my address; please let Eve have it. I shall call to-morrow morning again."

He did so, and this time found Eve, as well as her companion, ready to go out. No remark or inquiry concerning her health passed his lips; he saw that she was recovering from the crisis she had passed through, whatever its real nature. Eve shook hands with him, and smiled, though as if discharging an obligation.

"Can you spare time to show us something of Paris?" she asked.

"I am your official guide. Make use of me whenever it pleases you."

"I don't feel able to go very far. Isn't there some place where we could sit down in the open air?"

A carriage was summoned, and they drove to the Fields Elysian. Eve benefited by the morning thus spent. She left to Patty most of the conversation, but occasionally made inquiries, and began to regard things with a healthy interest. The next day they all visited the Louvre, for a light rain was falling, and here Hilliard found an opportunity of private talk with Eve; they sat together whilst Patty, who cared little for pictures, looked out of a window at the Seine.

"Do you like the hotel I chose?" he began.

"Everything is very nice."

"And you are not sorry to be here?"

"Not in one way. In another I can't understand how I come to be here at all."

"Your physician has ordered it."

"Yes—so I suppose it's all right."

"There's one thing I'm obliged to speak of. Do you understand French money?"

Eve averted her face, and spoke after a slight delay.

"I can easily learn."

"Yes. You shall take this Paris guide home with you. You'll find all information of that sort in it. And I shall give you an envelope containing money—just for your private use. You have nothing to do with the charges at the hotel."

"I've brought it on myself; but I feel more ashamed than I can tell you."

"If you tried to tell me I shouldn't listen. What you have to do now is to get well. Very soon you and Patty will be able to find your way about together; then I shall only come with you when you choose to invite me. You have my address."

He rose and broke off the dialogue.

For a week or more Eve's behaviour in his company underwent little change. In health she decidedly improved, but Hilliard always found her reserved, coldly amicable, with an occasional suggestion of forced humility which he much disliked. From Patty he learnt that she went about a good deal and seemed to enjoy herself.

"We don't always go together," said the girl. "Yesterday and the day before Eve was away by herself all the afternoon. Of course she can get on all right with her French. She takes to Paris as if she'd lived here for years."

On the day after, Hilliard received a postcard in which Eve asked him to be in a certain room of the Louvre at twelve o'clock. He kept the appointment, and found Eve awaiting him alone.

"I wanted to ask whether you would mind if we left the hotel and went to live at another place?"

He heard her with surprise.

"You are not comfortable?"

"Quite. But I have been to see my friend Mdlle. Roche—you remember. And she has shown me how we can live very comfortably at a quarter of what it costs now, in the same house where she has a room. I should like to change, if you'll let me."

"Pooh! You're not to think of the cost——"

"Whether I am to or not, I do, and can't help myself. I know the hotel is fearfully expensive, and I shall like the other place much better. Miss Roche is a very nice girl, and she was glad to see me; and if I'm near her, I shall get all sorts of advantages—in French, and so on."

Hilliard wondered what accounts of herself Eve had rendered to the Parisienne, but he did not venture to ask.

"Will Patty like it as well?"

"Just as well. Miss Roche speaks English, you know, and they'll get on very well together."

"Where is the place?"

"Rather far off—towards the Jardin des Plantes. But I don't think that would matter, would it?"

"I leave it entirely to you."

"Thank you," she answered, with that intonation he did not like. "Of course, if you would like to meet Miss Roche, you can."

"We'll think about it. It's enough that she's an old friend of yours."

## CHAPTER XV

When this change had been made Eve seemed to throw off a burden. She met Hilliard with something like the ease of manner, the frank friendliness, which marked her best moods in their earlier intercourse. At a restaurant dinner, to which he persuaded her in company with Patty, she was ready in cheerful talk, and an expedition to Versailles, some days after, showed her radiant with the joy of sunshine and movement. Hilliard could not but wonder at the success of his prescription.

He did not visit the girls in their new abode, and nothing more was said of his making the acquaintance of Mdlle. Roche. Meetings were appointed by post-card—always in Patty's hand if the initiative were female; they took place three or four times a week. As it was now necessary for Eve to make payments on her own account, Hilliard despatched to her by post a remittance in paper money, and of this no word passed between them. Three weeks later he again posted the same sum. On the morrow they went by river to St. Cloud—it was always a trio, Hilliard never making any other proposal—and the steam-boat afforded Eve an opportunity of speaking with her generous friend apart.

"I don't want this money," she said, giving him an envelope. "What you sent before isn't anything like finished. There's enough for a month more."

"Keep it all the same. I won't have any pinching."

"There's nothing of the kind. If I don't have my way in this I shall go back to London."

He put the envelope in his pocket, and stood silent, with eyes fixed on the river bank.

"How long do you intend us to stay?" asked Eve.

"As long as you find pleasure here."

"And—what am I to do afterwards?"

He glanced at her.

"A holiday must come to an end," she added, trying, but without success, to meet his look.

"I haven't given any thought to that," said Hilliard, carelessly; "there's plenty of time. It will be fine weather for many weeks yet."

"But I have been thinking about it. I should be crazy if I didn't."

"Tell me your thoughts, then."

"Should you be satisfied if I got a place at Birmingham?"

There again was the note of self-abasement. It irritated the listener.

"Why do you put it in that way? There's no question of what satisfies me, but of what is good for you."

"Then I think it had better be Birmingham."

"Very well. It's understood that when we leave Paris we go there."

A silence. Then Eve asked abruptly:

"You will go as well?"

"Yes, I shall go back."

"And what becomes of your determination to enjoy life as long as you can?"

"I'm carrying it out. I shall go back satisfied, at all events."

"And return to your old work?"

"I don't know. It depends on all sorts of things. We won't talk of it just yet."

Patty approached, and Hilliard turned to her with a bright, jesting face.

Midway in August, on his return home one afternoon, the concierge let him know that two English gentlemen had been inquiring for him; one of them had left a card. With surprise and pleasure Hilliard read the name of Robert Narramore, and beneath it, written in pencil, an invitation to dine that evening at a certain hotel in the Rue de Provence. As usual, Narramore had neglected the duties of a correspondent; this was the first announcement of his intention to be in Paris. Who the second man might be Hilliard could not conjecture.

He arrived at the hotel, and found Narramore in company with a man of about the same age, his name Birching, to Hilliard a stranger. They had reached Paris this morning, and would remain only for a day or two, as their purpose was towards the Alps.

"I couldn't stand this heat," remarked Narramore, who, in the very lightest of tourist garbs, sprawled upon a divan, and drank something iced out of a tall tumbler. "We shouldn't have stopped here at all if it hadn't been for you. The idea is that you should go on with us."

"Can't—impossible——"

"Why, what are you doing here—besides roasting?"

"Eating and drinking just what suits my digestion."

"You look pretty fit—a jolly sight better than when we met last. All the same, you will go on with us. We won't argue it now; it's dinner-time. Wait till afterwards."

At table, Narramore mentioned that his friend Birching was an architect.

"Just what this fellow ought to have been," he said, indicating Hilliard. "Architecture is his hobby. I believe he could sit down and draw to scale a front elevation of any great cathedral in Europe—couldn't you, Hilliard?"

Laughing the joke aside, Hilliard looked with interest at Mr. Birching, and began to talk with him. The three young men consumed a good deal of wine, and after dinner strolled about the streets, until Narramore's fatigue and thirst brought them to a pause at a café on the Boulevard des Italiens. Birching presently moved apart, to reach a newspaper, and remained out of earshot while Narramore talked with his other friend.

"What's going on?" he began. "What are you doing here? Seriously, I want you to go along with us. Birching is a very good sort of chap, but just a trifle heavy—takes things rather solemnly for such hot weather. Is it the expense? Hang it! You and I know each other well enough, and, thanks to my old uncle——"

"Never mind that, old boy," interposed Hilliard. "How long are you going for?"

"I can't very well be away for more than three weeks. The brass bedsteads, you know——"

Hilliard agreed to join in the tour.

"That's right: I've been looking forward to it," said his friend heartily. "And now, haven't you anything to tell me? Are you alone here? Then, what the deuce do you do with yourself?"

"Chiefly meditate."

"You're the rummest fellow I ever knew. I've wanted to write to you, but—hang it!—what with hot weather and brass bedsteads, and this and that—— Now, what *are* you going to do? Your money won't last for ever. Haven't you any projects? It was no good talking about it before you left Dudley. I saw that. You were all but fit for a lunatic asylum, and no wonder. But you've pulled round, I see. Never saw you looking in such condition. What is to be the next move?"

"I have no idea."

"Well, now, *I* have. This fellow Birching is partner with his brother, in Brum, and they're tolerably flourishing. I've thought of you ever since I came to know him; I think it was chiefly on your account that I got thick with him—though there was another reason: I'll tell you about that some time. Now, why shouldn't you go into their office? Could you manage to pay a small premium? I believe I

could square it with them. I haven't said anything. I never hurry—
like things to ripen naturally. Suppose you saw your way, in a year
or two, to make only as much in an architect's office as you did in
that——machine-shop, wouldn't it be worth while?"

Hilliard mused. Already he had a flush on his cheek, but his eyes
sensibly brightened.

"Yes," he said at length with deliberation. "It would be worth
while."

"So I should think. Well, wait till you've got to be a bit chummy
with Birching. I think you'll suit each other. Let him see that you do
really know something about architecture—there'll be plenty of
chances."

Hilliard, still musing, repeated with mechanical emphasis:

"Yes, it would be worth while."

Then Narramore called to Birching, and the talk became general
again.

The next morning they drove about Paris, all together. Narramore,
though it was his first visit to the city, declined to see anything which
demanded exertion, and the necessity for quenching his thirst recurred
with great frequency. Early in the afternoon he proposed that they
should leave Paris that very evening.

"I want to see a mountain with snow on it. We're bound to travel
by night, and another day of this would settle me. Any objection,
Birching?"

The architect agreed, and time-tables were consulted. Hilliard drove
home to pack. When this was finished, he sat down and wrote a letter:

Dear Miss Madeley,

My friend Narramore is here, and has persuaded me to go to Switzerland
with him. I shall be away for a week or two, and will let you hear from me in
the meantime. Narramore says I am looking vastly better, and it is you I have
to thank for this. Without you, my attempts at 'enjoying life' would have been
a poor business. We start in an hour or two,—Yours ever,

Maurice Hilliard.

## CHAPTER XVI

He was absent for full three weeks, and arrived with his friends at the
Gare de Lyon early one morning of September. Narramore and the
architect delayed only for a meal, and pursued their journey homeward; Hilliard returned to his old quarters despatched a post-card

asking Eve and Patty to dine with him that evening, and thereupon went to bed, where for some eight hours he slept the sleep of healthy fatigue.

The place he had appointed for meeting with the girls was at the foot of the Boulevard St. Michel. Eve came alone.

"And where's Patty?" he asked, grasping her hand heartily in return for the smile of unfeigned pleasure with which she welcomed him.

"Ah, where indeed? Getting near to Charing Cross by now, I think."

"She has gone back?"

"Went this very morning, before I had your card—let us get out of the way of people. She has been dreadfully home-sick. About a fortnight ago a mysterious letter came for her; she hid it away from me. A few days after another came, and she shut herself up for a long time, and when she came out again I saw she had been crying. Then we talked it over. She had written to Mr. Dally and got an answer that made her miserable; that was the *first* letter. She wrote again, and had a reply that made her still more wretched; and that was the *second*. Two or three more came, and yesterday she could bear it no longer."

"Then she has gone home to make it up with him?"

"Of course. He declared that she has utterly lost her character and that no honest man could have anything more to say to her! I shouldn't wonder if they are married in a few weeks' time."

Hilliard laughed light-heartedly.

"I was to beg you on my knees to forgive her," pursued Eve. "But I can't very well do that in the middle of the street, can I? Really, she thinks she has behaved disgracefully to you. She wouldn't write a letter—she was ashamed. 'Tell him to forget all about me!' she kept saying."

"Good little girl! And what sort of a husband will this fellow Dally make her?"

"No worse than husbands in general, I dare say—but how well you look! How you must have been enjoying yourself!"

"I can say exactly the same about you!"

"Oh, but you are sunburnt, and look quite a different man!"

"And you have an exquisite colour in your cheeks, and eyes twice as bright as they used to be; and one would think you had never known a care."

"I feel almost like that," said Eve, laughing.

He tried to meet her eyes; she eluded him.

"I have an Alpine hunger; where shall we dine?"

The point called for no long discussion, and presently they were seated in the cool restaurant. Whilst he nibbled an olive, Hilliard ran over the story of his Swiss tour.

"If only *you* had been there! It was the one thing lacking."

"You wouldn't have enjoyed yourself half so much. You amused me by your description of Mr. Narramore, in the letter from Geneva."

"The laziest rascal born! But the best-tempered, the easiest to live with. A thoroughly good fellow; I like him better than ever. Of course he is improved by coming in for money—who wouldn't be, that has any good in him at all? But it amazes me that he can be content to go back to Birmingham and his brass bedsteads. Sheer lack of energy, I suppose. He'll grow dreadfully fat, I fear, and by when he becomes really a rich man—it's awful to think of."

Eve asked many questions about Narramore; his image gave mirthful occupation to her fancy. The dinner went merrily on, and when the black coffee was set before them:

"Why not have it outside?" said Eve. "You would like to smoke, I know."

Hilliard assented, and they seated themselves under the awning. The boulevard glowed in a golden light of sunset; the sound of its traffic was subdued to a lulling rhythm.

"There's a month yet before the leaves will begin to fall," murmured the young man, when he had smoked awhile in silence.

"Yes," was the answer. "I shall be glad to have a little summer still in Birmingham."

"Do you wish to go?"

"I shall go to-morrow, or the day after," Eve replied quietly.

Then again there came silence.

"Something has been proposed to me," said Hilliard, at length, leaning forward with his elbows upon the table. "I mentioned that our friend Birching is an architect. He's in partnership with his brother, a much older man. Well, they have offered to take me into their office if I pay a premium of fifty guineas. As soon as I can qualify myself to be of use to them, they'll give me a salary. And I shall have the chance of eventually doing much better than I ever could at the old grind, where, in fact, I had no prospect whatever."

"That's very good news," Eve remarked, gazing across the street.

"You think I ought to accept?"

"I suppose you can pay the fifty guineas, and still leave yourself enough to live upon?"

"Enough till I earn something," Hilliard answered with a smile.

"Then I should think there's no doubt."

"The question is this—are you perfectly willing to go back to Birmingham?"

"I'm *anxious* to go."

"You feel quite restored to health?"

"I was never so well in my life."

Hilliard looked into her face, and could easily believe that she spoke the truth. His memory would no longer recall the photograph in Mrs. Brewer's album; the living Eve, with her progressive changes of countenance, had obliterated that pale image of her bygone self. He saw her now as a beautiful woman, mysterious to him still in many respects, yet familiar as though they had been friends for years.

"Then, whatever life is before me," he said, "I shall have done *one* thing that is worth doing."

"Perhaps—if everyone's life is worth saving," Eve answered in a voice just audible.

"Everyone's is not; but yours was."

Two men who had been sitting not far from them rose and walked away. As if more at her ease for this secession, Eve looked at her companion, and said in a tone of intimacy:

"How I must have puzzled you when you first saw me in London!"

He answered softly:

"To be sure you did. And the thought of it puzzles me still."

"Oh, but can't you understand? No; of course you can't—I have told you so little. Just give me an idea of what sort of person you expected to find."

"Yes, I will. Judging from your portrait, and from what I was told of you, I looked for a sad, solitary, hard-working girl—rather poorly dressed—taking no pleasure—going much to chapel—shrinking from the ordinary world."

"And you felt disappointed?"

"At first, yes; or, rather, bewildered—utterly unable to understand you."

"You are disappointed still?" she asked.

"I wouldn't have you anything but what you are."

"Still, that other girl was the one you *wished* to meet."

"Yes, before I had seen you. It was the sort of resemblance between her life and my own. I thought of sympathy between us. And the face of the portrait—but I see better things in the face that is looking at me now."

"Don't be quite sure of that—yes, perhaps. It's better to be healthy, and enjoy life, than broken-spirited and hopeless. The strange thing is that you were right—you fancied me just the kind of a girl I was: sad and solitary, and shrinking from people—true enough. And I went to chapel, and got comfort from it—as I hope to do again. Don't think that I have no religion. But I was so unhealthy, and suffered so in every way. Work and anxiety without cease, from when I was twelve years old. You know all about my father? If I hadn't been clever at figures, what would have become of me? I should have drudged at some wretched occupation until the work and the misery of everything killed me."

Hilliard listened intently, his eyes never stirring from her face.

"The change in me began when father came back to us, and I began to feel my freedom. Then I wanted to get away, and to live by myself. I thought of London—I've told you how much I always thought of London—but I hadn't the courage to go there. In Birmingham I began to change my old habits; but more in what I thought than what I did. I wished to enjoy myself like other girls, but I couldn't. For one thing, I thought it wicked; and then I was so afraid of spending a penny—I had so often known what it was to be in want of a copper to buy food. So I lived quite alone; sat in my room every evening and read books. You could hardly believe what a number of books I read in that year. Sometimes I didn't go to bed till two or three o'clock."

"What sort of books?"

"I got them from the Free Library—books of all kinds; not only novels. I've never been particularly fond of novels; they always made me feel my own lot all the harder. I never could understand what people mean when they say that reading novels takes them 'out of themselves.' It was never so with me. I liked travels and lives of people, and books about the stars. Why do you laugh?"

"You escaped from yourself *there*, at all events."

"At last I saw an advertisement in a newspaper—a London paper in the reading-room—which I was tempted to answer; and I got an engagement in London. When the time came for starting I was so afraid and low-spirited that I all but gave it up. I should have done, if I could have known what was before me. The first year in London was all loneliness and ill-health. I didn't make a friend, and I starved myself, all to save money. Out of my pound a week I saved several shillings—just because it was the habit of my whole life to pinch and pare and deny myself. I was obliged to dress decently, and that came out of my food. It's certain I must have a very good constitution to have gone through all that and be as well as I am to-day."

"It will never come again," said Hilliard.

"How can I be sure of that? I told you once before that I'm often in dread of the future. It would be ever so much worse, after knowing what it means to enjoy one's life. How do people feel who are quite sure they can never want as long as they live? I have tried to imagine it, but I can't; it would be too wonderful."

"You may know it some day."

Eve reflected.

"It was Patty Ringrose," she continued, "who taught me to take life more easily. I was astonished to find how much enjoyment she could get out of an hour or two of liberty, with sixpence to spend. She did me good by laughing at me, and in the end I astonished *her*. Wasn't it natural that I should be reckless as soon as I got the chance?"

"I begin to understand."

"The chance came in this way. One Sunday morning I went by myself to Hampstead, and as I was wandering about on the Heath I kicked against something. It was a cash-box, which I saw couldn't have been lying there very long. I found it had been broken open, and inside it were a lot of letters—old letters in envelopes; nothing else. The addresses on the envelopes were all the same—to a gentleman living at Hampstead. I thought the best I could do was to go and inquire for this address; and I found it, and rang the door-bell. When I told the servant what I wanted—it was a large house—she asked me to come in, and after I had waited a little she took me into a library, where a gentleman was sitting. I had to answer a good many questions, and the man talked rather gruffly to me. When he had made a note of my name and where I lived, he said that I should hear from him, and so I went away. Of course I hoped to have a reward, but for two or three days I heard nothing; then, when I was at business, someone asked to see me—a man I didn't know. He said he had come from Mr. So-and-So, the gentleman at Hampstead, and had brought something for me—four five-pound notes. The cash-box had been stolen by someone, with other things, the night before I found it, and the letters in it, which disappointed the thief, had a great value for their owner. All sorts of inquiries had been made about me, and no doubt I very nearly got into the hands of the police, but it was all right, and I had twenty pounds reward. Think! twenty pounds!"

Hilliard nodded.

"I told no one about it—not even Patty. And I put the money into the Post Office savings bank. I meant it to stay there till I might be in need; but I thought of it day and night. And only a fortnight after, my employers shut up their place of business, and I had nothing to do. All one night I lay awake, and when I got up in the morning I felt as if I was no longer my old self. I saw everything in a different way—felt altogether changed. I had made up my mind not to look for a new place, but to take my money out of the Post Office—I had more than twenty-five pounds there altogether—and spend it for my pleasure. It was just as if something had enraged me, and I was bent on avenging myself. All that day I walked about the town, looking at shops, and thinking what I should like to buy: but I only spent a shilling or two, for meals. The next day I bought some new clothing. The day after that I took Patty to the theatre, and astonished her by my extravagance; but I gave her no explanation, and to this day she doesn't understand how I got my money. In a sort of way, I *did* enjoy myself. For one thing, I took a subscription at Mudie's, and began to read once more. You can't think how it pleased me to get my books—new books—where rich people do. I changed a volume about every other day—I had so many hours I didn't know what to do with. Patty was the only friend I had made, so I took her about with me whenever she could get away in the evening."

"Yet never once dined at a restaurant," remarked Hilliard, laughing. "There's the difference between man and woman."

"My ideas of extravagance were very modest, after all."

Hilliard, fingering his coffee-cup, said in a lower voice:

"Yet you haven't told me everything."

Eve looked away, and kept silence.

"By the time I met you"—he spoke in his ordinary tone—"you had begun to grow tired of it."

"Yes—and——" She rose. "We won't sit here any longer."

When they had walked for a few minutes:

"How long shall you stay in Paris?" she asked.

"Won't you let me travel with you?"

"I do whatever you wish," Eve answered simply.

## CHAPTER XVII

Her accent of submission did not affect Hilliard as formerly; with a nervous thrill, he felt that she spoke as her heart dictated. In his absence Eve had come to regard him, if not with the feeling he desired, with something that resembled it; he read the change in her eyes. As they walked slowly away she kept nearer to him than of wont; now and then her arm touched his, and the contact gave him a delicious sensation. Askance he observed her figure, its graceful, rather languid, movement; to-night she had a new power over him, and excited with a passion which made his earlier desires seem spiritless.

"One day more of Paris?" he asked softly.

"Wouldn't it be better——?" she hesitated in the objection.

"Do you wish to break the journey in London?"

"No; let us go straight on."

"To-morrow, then?"

"I don't think we ought to put it off. The holiday is over."

Hilliard nodded with satisfaction. An incident of the street occupied them for a few minutes, and their serious conversation was only resumed when they had crossed to the south side of the river, where they turned eastwards and went along the quays.

"Till I can find something to do," Eve said at length, "I shall live at Dudley. Father will be very glad to have me there. He wished me to stay longer."

"I am wondering whether it is really necessary for you to go back to your drudgery."

"Oh, of course it is," she answered quickly. "I mustn't be idle. That's the very worst thing for me. And how am I to live?"

"I have still plenty of money," said Hilliard, regarding her.

"No more than you will need."

"But think—how little more it costs for two than for one——"

He spoke in spite of himself, having purposed no such suggestion. Eve quickened her step.

"No, no, no! You have a struggle before you; you don't know what——"

"And if it would make it easier for me?—there's no real doubt about my getting on well enough——"

"Everything is doubtful." She spoke in a voice of agitation. "We can't see a day before us. We have arranged everything very well——"

Hilliard was looking across the river. He walked more and more slowly, and turned at length to stand by the parapet. His companion remained apart from him, waiting. But he did not turn towards her again, and she moved to his side.

"I know how ungrateful I must seem." She spoke without looking at him. "I have no right to refuse anything after all you——"

"Don't say that," he interrupted impatiently. "That's the one thing I shall never like to think of."

"I shall think of it always, and be glad to remember it——"

"Come nearer—give me your hand——"

Holding it, he drew her against his side, and they stood in silence looking upon the Seine, now dark beneath the clouding night.

"I can't feel sure of you," fell at length from Hilliard.

"I promise——"

"Yes; here, now, in Paris. But when you are back in that hell——"

"What difference can it make in me? It can't change what I feel now. You have altered all my life, my thoughts about everything. When I look back, I don't know myself. You were right; I must have been suffering from an illness that affected my mind. It seems impossible that I could ever have done such things. I ought to tell you. Do you wish me to tell you everything?"

Hilliard spoke no answer, but he pressed her hand more tightly in his own.

"You knew it from Patty, didn't you?"

"She told me as much as she knew that night when I waited for you in High Street. She said you were in danger, and I compelled her to tell all she could."

"I *was* in danger, though I can't understand now how it went so far as that. It was he who came to me with the money, from the

gentleman at Hampstead. That was how I first met him. The next day
he waited for me when I came away from business.''

"It was the first time that anything of that kind had happened?''

"The first time. And you know what the state of my mind was then.
But to the end I never felt any—I never really loved him. We met and
went to places together. After my loneliness—you can understand. But
I distrusted him. Did Patty tell you why I left London so suddenly?''

"Yes.''

"When that happened I knew my instinct had been right from the
first. It gave me very little pain, but I was ashamed and disgusted. He
hadn't tried to deceive me in words; he never spoke of marriage; and
from what I found out then, I saw that he was very much to be
pitied.''

"You seem to contradict yourself," said Hilliard. "Why were you
ashamed and disgusted?''

"At finding myself in the power of such a woman. He married her
when she was very young, and I could imagine the life he had led with
her until he freed himself. A hateful woman!''

"Hateful to you, I see," muttered the listener, with something tight
at his heart.

"Not because I felt anything like jealousy. You must believe me. I
should never have spoken if I hadn't meant to tell you the simple
truth.''

Again he pressed her hand. The warmth of her body had raised his
blood to fever-heat.

"When we met again, after I came back, it was by chance. I refused
to speak to him, but he followed me all along the street, and I didn't
know it till I was nearly home. Then he came up again, and implored
me to hear what he had to say. I knew he would wait for me again in
High Street, so I had no choice but to listen, and then tell him that
there couldn't be anything more between us. And, for all that, he
followed me another day. And again I had to listen to him.''

Hilliard fancied that he could feel her heart beat against his arm.

"Be quick!" he said. "Tell all, and have done with it.''

"He told me, at last, that he was ruined. His wife had brought him
into money difficulties; she ran up bills that he was obliged to pay,
and left him scarcely enough to live upon. And he had used money
that was not his own—he would have to give an account of it in a day
or two. He was trying to borrow, but no one would lend him half
what he needed——''

"That's enough," Hilliard broke in, as her voice became inaudible.

"No, you ought to know more than I have told you. Of course he
didn't ask me for money; he had no idea that I could lend him even a

pound. But what I wish you to know is that he hadn't spoken to me
again in the old way. He said he had done wrong, when he first came
to know me; he begged me to forgive him that, and only wanted me to
be his friend.''

''Of course.''

''Oh, don't be ungenerous: that's so unlike you.''

''I didn't mean it ungenerously. In his position I should have done
exactly as he did.''

''Say you believe me. There was not a word of love between us. He
told me all about the miseries of his life—that was all; and I pitied
him so. I felt he was so sincere.''

''I believe it perfectly.''

''There was no excuse for what I did. How I had the courage—the
shamelessness—is more than I can understand now.''

Hilliard stirred himself, and tried to laugh.

''As it turned out, you couldn't have done better. Well, there's an
end of it. Come.''

He walked on, and Eve kept closely beside him, looking up into his
face.

''I am sure he will pay the money back,'' she said presently.

''Hang the money!''

Then he stood still.

''How is he to pay it back? I mean, how is he to communicate with
you?''

''I gave him my address at Dudley.''

Again Hilliard moved on.

''Why should it annoy you?'' Eve asked. ''If ever he writes to me, I
shall let you know at once: you shall see the letter. It is quite certain
that he *will* pay his debt; and I shall be very glad when he does.''

''What explanation did you give him?''

''The true one. I said I had borrowed from a friend. He was in
despair, and couldn't refuse what I offered.''

''We'll talk no more of it. It was right to tell me. I'm glad now it's
all over. Look at the moon rising—harvest moon, isn't it?''

Eve turned aside again, and leaned on the parapet. He, lingering
apart for a moment, at length drew nearer. Of her own accord she put
her hands in his.

''In future,'' she said, ''you shall know everything I do. You can
trust me: there will be no more secrets.''

''Yet you are afraid——''

''It's for your sake. You must be free for the next year or two. I
shall be glad to get to work again. I am well and strong and cheerful.''

Her eyes drew him with the temptation he had ever yet resisted.
Eve did not refuse her lips.

"You must write to Patty," she said, when they were at the place of parting. "I shall have her new address in a day or two."

"Yes, I will write to her."

## CHAPTER XVIII

By the end of November Hilliard was well at work in the office of Messrs. Birching, encouraged by his progress and looking forward as hopefully as a not very sanguine temperament would allow. He lived penuriously, and toiled at professional study night as well as day. Now and then he passed an evening with Robert Narramore, who had moved to cozy bachelor quarters a little distance out of town, in the Halesowen direction. Once a week, generally on Saturday, he saw Eve. Other society he had none, nor greatly desired any.

But Eve had as yet found no employment. Good fortune in this respect seemed to have deserted her, and at her meetings with Hilliard she grew fretful over repeated disappointments. Of her day-to-day life she made no complaint, but Hilliard saw too clearly that her spirits were failing beneath a burden of monotonous dulness. That the healthy glow she had brought back in her cheeks should give way to pallor was no more than he had expected, but he watched with anxiety the return of mental symptoms which he had tried to cheat himself into believing would not reappear. Eve did not fail in pleasant smiles, in hopeful words; but they cost her an effort which she lacked the art to conceal. He felt a coldness in her, divined a struggle between conscience and inclination. However, for this also he was prepared; all the more need for vigour and animation on his own part.

Hilliard had read of the woman who, in the strength of her love and loyalty, heartens a man through all the labours he must front; he believed in her existence, but had never encountered her—as indeed very few men have. From Eve he looked for nothing of the kind. If she would permit herself to rest upon his sinews, that was all he desired. The mood of their last night in Paris might perchance return, but only with like conditions. Of his workaday passion she knew nothing; habit of familiarity and sense of obligation must supply its place with her until a brightening future once more set her emotions to the gladsome tune.

Now that the days of sun and warmth were past, it was difficult to arrange for a meeting under circumstances that allowed of free comfortable colloquy. Eve declared that her father's house offered no sort of convenience; it was only a poor cottage, and Hilliard would be altogether out of place there. To his lodgings she could not come. Of necessity they had recourse to public places in Birmingham, where an hour or two of talk under shelter might make Eve's journey hither worth while. As Hilliard lived at the north end of the town, he suggested Aston Hall as a possible rendezvous, and here they met, early one Saturday afternoon in December.

From the eminence which late years have encompassed with a proletarian suburb, its once noble domain narrowed to the bare acres of a stinted breathing ground, Aston Hall looks forth upon joyless streets and fuming chimneys, a wide welter of squalid strife. Its walls, which bear the dints of Roundhead cannonade, are blackened with ever-driving smoke; its crumbling gateway, opening aforetime upon a stately avenue of chestnuts, shakes as the steam-tram rushes by. Hilliard's imagination was both attracted and repelled by this relic of what he deemed a better age. He enjoyed the antique chambers, the winding staircases, the lordly gallery, with its dark old portraits and vast fireplaces, the dim-lighted nooks where one could hide alone and dream away the present; but in the end, reality threw scorn upon such pleasure. Aston Hall was a mere architectural relic, incongruous and meaningless amid its surroundings; the pathos of its desecrated dignity made him wish that it might be destroyed, and its place fittingly occupied by some People's Palace, brand new, aglare with electric light, ringing to the latest melodies of the street. When he had long gazed at its gloomy front, the old champion of royalism seemed to shrink together, humiliated by Time's insults.

It was raining when he met Eve at the entrance.

"This won't do," were his first words. "You can't come over in such weather as this. If it hadn't seemed to be clearing up an hour or two ago, I should have telegraphed to stop you."

"Oh, the weather is nothing to me," Eve answered, with resolute gaiety. "I'm only too glad of the change. Besides, it won't go on much longer. I shall get a place."

Hilliard never questioned her about her attempts to obtain an engagement; the subject was too disagreeable to him.

"Nothing yet," she continued, as they walked up the muddy roadway to the Hall. "But I know you don't like to talk about it."

"I have something to propose. How if I take a couple of cheap rooms in some building let out for offices, and put in a few sticks of furniture? Would you come to see me there?"

He watched her face as she listened to the suggestion, and his timidity seemed justified by her expression.

"You would be so uncomfortable in such a place. Don't trouble. We shall manage to meet somehow. I am certain to be living here before long."

"Even when you are," he persisted, "we shall only be able to see each other in places like this. I can't talk—can't say half the things I wish to——"

"We'll think about it. Ah, it's warm in here!"

This afternoon the guardians of the Hall were likely to be troubled with few visitors. Eve at once led the way upstairs to a certain suite of rooms, hung with uninteresting pictures, where she and Hilliard had before this spent an hour safe from disturbance. She placed herself in the recess of a window: her companion took a few steps backward and forward.

"Let me do what I wish," he urged. "There's a whole long winter before us. I am sure I could find a couple of rooms at a very low rent, and some old woman would come in to do all that's necessary."

"If you like."

"I may? You would come there?" he asked eagerly.

"Of course I would come. But I sha'n't like to see you in a bare, comfortless place."

"It needn't be that. A few pounds will make a decent sort of sitting-room."

"Anything to tell me?" Eve asked, abruptly quitting the subject.

She seemed to be in better spirits than of late, notwithstanding the evil sky; and Hilliard smiled with pleasure as he regarded her.

"Nothing unusual. Oh, yes; I'm forgetting. I had a letter from Emily, and went to see her."

Hilliard had scarcely seen his quondam sister-in-law since she became Mrs. Marr. On the one occasion of his paying a call, after his return from Paris, it struck him that her husband offered no very genial welcome. He had expected this, and willingly kept aloof.

"Read the letter."

Eve did so. It began, "My dear Maurice," and ended, "Ever affectionately and gratefully yours." The rest of its contents ran thus:

"I am in great trouble—dreadfully unhappy. It would be such a kindness if you would let me see you. I can't put in a letter what I want to say, and I do hope you won't refuse to come. Friday afternoon, at three, would do, if you can get away from business for once. How I look back on the days when you used to come over from Dudley and have tea with us in the dear little room. Do come!"

"Of course," said Hilliard, laughing as he met Eve's surprised look. "I knew what *that* meant. I would much rather have got out of it, but it would have seemed brutal. So I went. The poor simpleton has begun to find that marriage with one man isn't necessarily the same thing as marriage with another. In Ezra Marr she has caught a Tartar."

"Surely he doesn't ill-use her?"

"Not a bit of it. He is simply a man with a will, and finds it necessary to teach his wife her duties. Emily knows no more about the duties of life than her little five-year-old girl. She thought she could play with a second husband as she did with the first, and she was gravely mistaken. She complained to me of a thousand acts of tyranny—every one of them, I could see, merely a piece of rude common-sense. The man must be calling himself an idiot for marrying her. I could only listen with a long face. Argument with Emily is out of the question. And I shall take good care not to go there again."

Eve asked many questions, and approved his resolve.

"You are not the person to console and instruct her. But she must look upon you as the best and wisest of men. I can understand that."

"You can understand poor, foolish Emily thinking so——"

"Put all the meaning you like into my words," said Eve, with her pleasantest smile. "Well, I too have had a letter. From Patty. She isn't going to be married, after all."

"Why, I thought it was over by now."

"She broke it off less than a week before the day. I wish I could show you her letter, but, of course, I mustn't. It's very amusing. They had quarrelled about every conceivable thing—all but one, and this came up at last. They were talking about meals, and Mr. Dally said that he liked a bloater for breakfast every morning. 'A bloater!' cried Patty. 'Then I hope you won't ask me to cook it for you. I can't bear them.' 'Oh, very well: if you can't cook a bloater, you're not the wife for me.' And there they broke off, for good and all."

"Which means for a month or two, I suppose."

"Impossible to say. But I have advised her as strongly as I could not to marry until she knows her own mind better. It is too bad of her to have gone so far. The poor man had taken rooms, and all but furnished them. Patty's a silly girl, I'm afraid."

"Wants a strong man to take her in hand—like a good many other girls."

Eve paid no attention to the smile.

"Paris spoilt her for such a man as Mr. Dally. She got all sorts of new ideas, and can't settle down to the things that satisfied her before. It isn't nice to think that perhaps we did her a great deal of harm."

"Nonsense! Nobody was ever harmed by healthy enjoyment."

"Was it healthy—for *her*? That's the question."

Hilliard mused, and felt disinclined to discuss the matter.

"That isn't the only news I have for you," said Eve presently. "I've had another letter."

Her voice arrested Hilliard's step as he paced near her.

"I had rather not have told you anything about it, but I promised.

And I have to give you something."

She held out to him a ten-pound note.

"What's this?"

"He has sent it. He says he shall be able to pay something every three months until he has paid the whole debt. Please to take it."

After a short struggle with himself, Hilliard recovered a manly bearing.

"It's quite right he should return the money, Eve, but you mustn't ask me to have anything to do with it. Use it for your own expenses. I gave it to you, and I can't take it back."

She hesitated, her eyes cast down.

"He has written a long letter. There's not a word in it I should be afraid to show you. Will you read it—just to satisfy me? Do read it!"

Hilliard steadily refused, with perfect self-command.

"I trust you—that's enough. I have absolute faith in you. Answer his letter in the way you think best, and never speak to me of the money again. It's yours; make what use of it you like."

"Then I shall use it," said Eve, after a pause, "to pay for a lodging in Birmingham. I couldn't live much longer at home. If I'm here, I can get books out of the library, and time won't drag so. And I shall be near you."

"Do so, by all means."

As if more completely to dismiss the unpleasant subject, they walked into another room. Hilliard began to speak again of his scheme for providing a place where they could meet and talk at their ease. Eve now entered into it with frank satisfaction.

"Have you said anything yet to Mr. Narramore?" she asked at length.

"No. I have never felt inclined to tell him. Of course I shall some day. But it isn't natural to me to talk of this kind of thing, even with so intimate a friend. Some men couldn't keep it to themselves: for me the difficulty is to speak."

"I asked again, because I have been thinking—mightn't Mr. Narramore be able to help me to get work?"

Hilliard repelled the suggestion with strong distaste. On no account would he seek his friend's help in such a matter. And Eve said no more of it.

On her return journey to Dudley, between eight and nine o'clock, she looked cold and spiritless. Her eyelids dropped wearily as she sat in the corner of the carriage with some papers on her lap, which Hilliard had given her. Rain had ceased, and the weather seemed turning to frost. From Dudley station she had a walk of nearly half an hour, to the top of Kate's Hill.

Kate's Hill is covered with an irregular assemblage of old red-tiled cottages, grimy without, but sometimes, as could be seen through an open door admitting into the chief room, clean and homely-looking within. The steep, narrow alleys leading upward were scarce lighted; here and there glimmered a pale corner-lamp, but on a black night such as this the oil-lit windows of a little shop, and the occasional gleam from doors, proved very serviceable as a help in picking one's path. Towards the top of the hill there was no paving, and mud lay thick. Indescribable the confusion of this toilers' settlement—houses and workshops tumbled together as if by chance, the ways climbing and winding into all manner of pitch-dark recesses, where cats prowled stealthily. In one spot silence and not a hint of life; in another, children noisily at play amid piles of old metal or miscellaneous rubbish. From the labyrinth which was so familiar to her, Eve issued of a sudden on to a sort of terrace, where the air blew shrewdly: beneath lay cottage roofs, and in front a limitless gloom, which by daylight would have been an extensive northward view, comprising the towns of Bilston and Wolverhampton. It was now a black gulf, without form and void, sputtering fire. Flames that leapt out of nothing, and as suddenly disappeared; tongues of yellow or of crimson, quivering, lambent, seeming to snatch and devour and then fall back in satiety. When a cluster of these fires shot forth together, the sky above became illumined with a broad glare, which throbbed and pulsed in the manner of sheet-lightning, though more lurid, and in a few seconds was gone.

She paused here for a moment, rather to rest after her climb than to look at what she had seen so often, then directed her steps to one of the houses within sight. She pushed the door, and entered a little parlour, where a fire and a lamp made cheery welcome. By the hearth, in a round-backed wooden chair, sat a grizzle-headed man, whose hard features proclaimed his relation to Eve, otherwise seeming so improbable. He looked up from the volume open on his knee—a Bible—and said in a rough, kind voice:

"I was thinkin' it 'ud be about toime for you. You look starved, my lass."

"Yes; it has turned very cold."

"I've got a bit o' supper ready for you. I don't want none myself; there's food enough for me *here*." He laid his hand on the book. "D' you call to mind the eighteenth of Ezekiel, lass?—'But if the wicked will turn from all his sins that he hath committed——'"

Eve stood motionless till he had read the verse, then nodded and began to take off her out-of-door garments. She was unable to talk, and her eyes wandered absently.

## CHAPTER XIX

After a week's inquiry, Hilliard discovered the lodging that would suit his purpose. It was Camp Hill; two small rooms at the top of a house, the ground-floor of which was occupied as a corn-dealer's shop, and the story above that tenanted by a working optician with a blind wife. On condition of papering the rooms and doing a few repairs necessary to make them habitable, he secured them at the low rent of four shillings a week.

Eve paid her first visit to this delectable abode on a Sunday afternoon; she saw only the sitting-room, which would bear inspection; the appearance of the bed-room was happily left to her surmise. Less than a five-pound note had paid for the whole furnishing. Notwithstanding the reckless invitation to Eve to share his fortunes straightway, Hilliard, after paying his premium of fifty guineas to the Birching Brothers, found but a very small remnant in hand of the money with which he had set forth from Dudley some nine months ago. Yet not for a moment did he repine; he had the value of his outlay; his mind was stored with memories and his heart strengthened with hope.

At her second coming—she herself now occupied a poor little lodging not very far away—Eve beheld sundry improvements. By the fireside stood a great leather chair, deep, high-backed, wondrously self-assertive over against the creaky cane seat which before had dominated the room. Against the wall was a high bookcase, where Hilliard's volumes, previously piled on the floor, stood in loose array; and above the mantelpiece hung a framed engraving of the Parthenon.

"This is dreadful extravagance!" she exclaimed, pausing at the threshold, and eying her welcomer with mock reproof.

"It is, but not on my part. The things came a day or two ago, simply addressed to me from shops."

"Who was the giver, then?"

"Must be Narramore, of course. He was here not long ago, and growled a good deal because I hadn't a decent chair for his lazy bones."

"I am much obliged to him," said Eve, as she sank back in the seat of luxurious repose. "You ought to hang his portrait in the room. Haven't you a photograph?" she added carelessly.

"Such a thing doesn't exist. Like myself, he hasn't had a portrait taken since he was a child. A curious thing, by-the-bye, that you should have had yours taken just when you did. Of course it was because you were going far away for the first time; but it marked a point in your life, and put on record the Eve Madeley whom no one would see again. If I can't get that photograph in any other way I shall go and buy, beg, or steal it from Mrs. Brewer."

"Oh, you shall have one if you insist upon it."

"Why did you refuse it before?"

"I hardly know—a fancy—I thought you would keep looking at it, and regretting that I had changed so."

As on her previous visit, she soon ceased to talk, and, in listening to Hilliard, showed unconsciously a tired, despondent face.

"Nothing yet," fell from her lips, when he had watched her silently.

"Never mind; I hate the mention of it."

"By-the-bye," he resumed, "Narramore astounded me by hinting at marriage. It's Miss Birching, the sister of my man. It hasn't come to an engagement yet, and if it ever does I shall give Miss Birching the credit for it. It would have amused you to hear him talking about her, with a pipe in his mouth and half asleep. I understand now why he took young Birching with him to Switzerland. He'll never carry it through; unless, as I said, Miss Birching takes the decisive step."

"Is she the kind of girl to do that?" asked Eve, waking to curiosity.

"I know nothing about her, except from Narramore's sleepy talk. Rather an arrogant beauty, according to him. He told me a story of how, when he was calling upon her, she begged him to ring the bell for something or other, and he was so slow in getting up that she went and rang it herself. 'Her own fault,' he said; 'she asked me to sit on a chair with a seat some six inches above the ground, and how can a man hurry up from a thing of that sort?'"

"He must be a strange man. Of course he doesn't care anything about Miss Birching."

"But I think he does, in his way."

"How did he ever get on at all in business?"

"Oh, he's one of the lucky men." Hilliard replied, with a touch of good-natured bitterness. "He never exerted himself; good things fell into his mouth. People got to like him—that's one explanation, no doubt."

"Don't you think he may have more energy than you imagine?"

"It's possible. I have sometimes wondered."

"What sort of life does he lead? Has he many friends I mean?"

"Very few. I should doubt whether there's anyone he talks with as he does with me. He'll never get much good out of his money; but if he fell into real poverty—poverty like mine—it would kill him. I know he looks at me as an astonishing creature, and marvels that I don't buy a good dose of chloral and have done with it."

Eve did not join in his laugh.

"I can't bear to hear you speak of your poverty," she said in an undertone. "You remind me that I am the cause of it."

"Good Heavens! As if I should mention it if I were capable of such a thought!"

"But it's the fact," she persisted, with something like irritation. "But for me, you would have gone into the architect's office with enough to live upon comfortably for a time."

"That's altogether unlikely," Hilliard declared. "But for you, it's improbable that I should have gone to Birching's at all. At this moment I should be spending my money in idleness, and, in the end, should have gone back to what I did before. You have given me a start in a new life."

This, and much more of the same tenor, failed to bring a light upon Eve's countenance. At length she asked suddenly, with a defiant bluntness——

"Have you ever thought what sort of a wife I am likely to make?"

Hilliard tried to laugh, but was disagreeably impressed by her words and the look that accompanied them.

"I have thought about it, to be sure," he answered carelessly.

"And don't you feel a need of courage?"

"Of course. And not only the need but the courage itself."

"Tell me the real, honest truth." She bent forward, and gazed at him with eyes one might have thought hostile. "I demand the truth of you: I have a right to know it. Don't you often wish you had never seen me?"

"You're in a strange mood."

"Don't put me off. Answer!"

"To ask such a question," he replied quietly, "is to charge me with a great deal of hypocrisy. I did *once* all but wish I had never seen you. If I lost you now I should lose what seems to me the strongest desire of my life. Do you suppose I sit down and meditate on your capacity as cook or housemaid? It would be very prudent and laudable, but I have other thoughts—that give me trouble enough."

"What thoughts?"

"Such as one doesn't talk about—if you insist on frankness."

Her eyes wandered.

"It's only right to tell you," she said, after silence, "that I dread poverty as much as ever I did. And I think poverty in marriage a thousand times worse than when one is alone."

"Well, we agree in that. But why do you insist upon it just now? Are *you* beginning to be sorry that we ever met?"

"Not a day passes but I feel sorry for it."

"I suppose you are harping on the old scruple. Why will you plague me about it?"

"I mean," said Eve, with eyes down, "that you are the worse off for having met me, but I mean something else as well. Do you think it possible that anyone can owe too much gratitude, even to a person one likes?"

He regarded her attentively.

"You feel the burden?"

She delayed her answer, glancing at him with a new expression—a deprecating tenderness.

"It's better to tell you. I *do* feel it, and have always felt it."

"Confound this infernal atmosphere!" Hilliard broke out wrathfully. "It's making you morbid again. Come here to me! Eve—come!"

As she sat motionless, he caught her hands and drew her forward, and sat down again with her passive body resting upon his knees. She was pale, and looked frightened.

"Your gratitude be hanged! Pay me back with your lips—so—and so! Can't you understand that when my lips touch yours, I have a delight that would be well purchased with years of semi-starvation? What is it to me how I won you? You are mine for good and all— that's enough."

She drew herself half away, and stood brightly flushed, touching her hair to set it in order again. Hilliard, with difficulty controlling himself, said in a husky voice——

"Is the mood gone?"

Eve nodded, and sighed.


# CHAPTER XX


At the time appointed for their next meeting, Hilliard waited in vain. An hour passed, and Eve, who had the uncommon virtue of punctuality, still did not come. The weather was miserable—rain, fog, and slush—but this had heretofore proved no obstacle, for her lodgings were situated less than half a mile away. Afraid of missing her if he went out, he fretted through another hour, and was at length relieved by the arrival of a letter of explanation. Eve wrote that she had been summoned to Dudley; her father was stricken with alarming illness, and her brother had telegraphed.

For two days he heard nothing; then came a few lines which told him that Mr. Madeley could not live many more hours. On the morrow Eve wrote that her father was dead.

To the letter which he thereupon despatched Hilliard had no reply for nearly a week. When Eve wrote, it was from a new address at Dudley. After thanking him for the kind words with which he had sought to comfort her, she continued——

"I have at last found something to do, and it was quite time, for I have been very miserable, and work is the best thing for me. Mr. Welland, my first employer, when I was twelve years old, has asked me to come and keep his books for him, and I am to live in his house. My brother has gone into lodgings, and we see no more of the cottage on Kate's Hill. It's a pity I have to be so far from you again, but there seems to be no hope of getting anything to do in Birmingham, and here I shall be comfortable enough, as far as mere living goes. On Sunday I shall be quite free, and will come over as often as possible; but I have caught a bad cold, and must be content to keep in the house until this dreadful weather changes. Be more careful of yourself than you generally are, and let me hear often. In a few months' time we shall be able to spend pleasant hours on the Castle Hill. I have heard from Patty, and want to tell you about her letter, but this cold makes me feel too stupid. Will write again soon."

It happened that Hilliard himself was just now blind and voiceless with a catarrh. The news from Dudley by no means solaced him. He crouched over his fire through the long, black day, tormented with many miseries, and at eventide drank half a bottle of whisky, piping hot, which at least assured him of a night's sleep.

Just to see what would be the result of his silence, he wrote no reply to this letter. A fortnight elapsed; he strengthened himself in stubbornness, aided by the catarrh, which many bottles of whisky would not overcome. When his solitary confinement grew at length insufferable, he sent for Narramore, and had not long to wait before his friend appeared. Narramore was rosy as ever: satisfaction with life beamed from his countenance.

"I've ordered you in some wine," he exclaimed genially, sinking into the easy-chair which Hilliard had vacated for him—an instance of selfishness in small things which did not affect his generosity in greater. "It isn't easy to get good port nowadays, but they tell me that this is not injurious. Hasn't young Birching been to see you? No, I suppose he would think it *infra dig.* to come to this neighbourhood. There's a damnable self-conceit in that family: you must have noticed it, eh? It comes out very strongly in the girl. By-the-bye, I've done with her—haven't been there for three weeks, and don't think I shall go again, unless it's for the pleasure of saying or doing something that'll irritate her royal highness."

"Did you quarrel?"

"Quarrel? I never quarrel with anyone; it's bad for one's nerves."

"Did you get as far as proposing?"

"Oh, I left *her* to do that. Women are making such a row about their rights nowadays, that it's as well to show you grant them perfect equality. I gave her every chance of saying something definite. I main-

tain that she trifled with my affections. She asked me what my views
in life were. Ah, thought I, now it's coming; and I answered modestly
that everything depended on circumstances. I might have said it
depended on the demand for brass bedsteads; but perhaps that would
have verged on indelicacy—you know that I am delicacy personified.
'I thought,' said Miss Birching, 'that a man of any energy made his
own circumstances?' 'Energy!' I shouted. 'Do you look for energy in
*me?* It's the greatest compliment anyone ever paid me.' At that she
seemed desperately annoyed, and wouldn't pursue the subject. That's
how it always was, just when the conversation grew interesting."

"I'm sorry to see you so cut up about it," remarked Hilliard.

"None of your irony, old fellow. Well, the truth is, I've seen
someone I like better."

"Not surprised."

"It's a queer story; I'll tell it you some day, if it comes to anything.
I'm not at all sure that it will, as there seems to be a sort of lurking
danger that I may make a damned fool of myself."

"Improbable?" commented the listener. "Your blood is too
temperate."

"So I thought; but one never knows. Unexpected feelings crop up in
a fellow. We won't talk about it just now. How have things been
going in the architectural line?"

"Not amiss. Steadily, I think."

Narramore lay back at full length, his face turned to the ceiling.

"Since I've been living out yonder, I've got a taste for the country. I
have a notion that, if brass bedsteads keep firm, I shall some day build
a little house of my own; an inexpensive little house, with a tree or
two about it. Just make me a few sketches, will you? When you've
nothing better to do, you know."

He played with the idea, till it took strong hold of him, and he
began to talk with most unwonted animation.

"Five or six thousand pounds—I ought to be able to sink that in a
few years. Not enough, eh? But I don't want a mansion. I'm quite
serious about this, Hilliard. When you're feeling ready to start on
your own account, you shall have the job."

Hilliard laughed grimly at the supposition that he would ever attain
professional independence, but his friend talked on, and overleaped
difficulties with a buoyancy of spirit which ultimately had its effect
upon the listener. When he was alone again, Hilliard felt better, both
in body and mind, and that evening, over the first bottle of Narramore's port, he amused himself with sketching ideal cottages.

"The fellow's in love, at last. When a man thinks of pleasant little
country houses, 'with a tree or two' about them——"

He sighed, and ground his teeth, and sketched on.

Before bedtime, a sudden and profound shame possessed him. Was
he not behaving outrageously in neglecting to answer Eve's letter? For
all he knew the cold of which she complained might have caused her
more suffering than he himself had gone through from the like cause,
and that was bad enough. He seized paper and wrote to her as he had
never written before, borne on the very high flood of passionate long-
ing. Without regard to prudence he left the house at midnight and
posted his letter.

"It never occurred to me to blame you for not writing," Eve quickly
replied; "I'm afraid you are more sensitive than I am, and, to tell the
truth, I believe men generally *are* more sensitive than women in things
of this kind. It pleased me very much to hear of the visit you had had
from Mr. Narramore, and that he had cheered you. I do so wish I
could have come, but I have really been quite ill, and I must not think
of risking a journey till the weather improves. Don't trouble about it;
I will write often.

"I told you about a letter I had had from poor Patty, and I want to
ask you to do something. Will you write to her? Just a nice, friendly
little letter. She would be *so* delighted, she would indeed. There's no
harm in copying a line or two from what she sent me. 'Has Mr.
Hilliard forgotten all about me?' she says. 'I would write to him, but I
feel afraid. Not afraid of *you,* dear Eve, but he might feel I was
impertinent. What do you think? We had such delicious times
together, he and you and I, and I really don't want him to forget me
altogether?' Now I have told her that there is no fear whatever of your
forgetting her, and that we often speak of her. I begin to think that I
have been unjust to Patty in calling her silly, and making fun of her.
She was anything but foolish in breaking off with that absurd Mr.
Dally, and I can see now that she will never give a thought to him
again. What I fear is that the poor girl will never find any one good
enough for her. The men she meets are very vulgar, and vulgar Patty
is *not*—as you once said to me, you remember. So, if you can spare a
minute, write her a few lines, to show that you still think of her. Her
address is——, etc."

To Hilliard all this seemed merely a pleasant proof of Eve's ami-
ability, of her freedom from that acrid monopolism which characterises
the ignoble female in her love relations. Straightway he did as he was
requested, and penned to Miss Ringrose a chatty epistle, with which
she could not but be satisfied. A day or two brought him an answer.
Patty's handwriting lacked distinction, and in the matter of
orthography she was not beyond reproach, but her letter chirped with
a prettily expressed gratitude. "I am living with my aunt, and am
likely to for a long time. And I get on very well at my new shop,
which I have no wish to leave." This was her only allusion to the

shattered matrimonial project: "I wish there was any chance of you and Eve coming to live in London, but I suppose that's too good to hope for. We don't get many things as we wish them in this world. And yet I oughtn't to say that either, for if it hadn't been for you I should never have seen Paris, which was so awfully jolly! But you'll be coming for a holiday, won't you? I should so like just to see you, if ever you do. It isn't like it was at the old shop. There's a great deal of business done here, and very little time to talk to anyone in the shop. But many girls have worse things to put up with than I have, and I won't make you think I'm a grumbler."

The whole of January went by before Hilliard and Eve again saw each other. The lover wrote at length that he could bear it no longer, that he was coming to Dudley, if only for the mere sight of Eve's face; she must meet him in the waiting-room at the railway station. She answered by return of post, "I will come over next Sunday, and be with you at twelve o'clock, but I must leave very early, as I am afraid to be out after nightfall." And this engagement was kept.

The dress of mourning became her well; it heightened her always noticeable air of refinement, and would have constrained to a reverential tenderness even had not Hilliard naturally checked himself from any bolder demonstration of joy. She spoke in a low, soft voice, seldom raised her eyes, and manifested a new gentleness very touching to Hilliard, though at the same time, and he knew not how or why, it did not answer to his desire. A midday meal was in readiness for her; she pretended to eat, but in reality scarce touched the food.

"You must taste old Narramore's port wine," said her entertainer. "The fellow actually sent a couple of dozen."

She was not to be persuaded; her refusal puzzled and annoyed Hilliard, and there followed a long silence. Indeed, it surprised him to find how little they could say to each other to-day. An unknown restraint had come between them.

"Well," he exclaimed at length, "I wrote to Patty, and she answered."

"May I see the letter?"

"Of course. Here it is."

Eve read it, and smiled with pleasure.

"Doesn't she write nicely! Poor girl!"

"Why have you taken so to commiserating her all at once?" Hilliard asked. "She's no worse off than she ever was. Rather better, I think."

"Life isn't the same for her since she was in Paris," said Eve, with peculiar softness.

"Well, perhaps it improved her."

"Oh, it certainly did! But it gave her a feeling of discontent for the old life and the people about her."

"A good many of us have to suffer that. She's nothing like as badly off as you are, my dear girl."

Eve coloured, and kept silence.

"We shall hear of her getting married before long," resumed the other. "She told me herself that marriage was the scourge of music-shops—it carries off their young women at such a rate."

"She told you that? It was in one of your long talks together in London? Patty and you got on capitally together. It was very natural she shouldn't care much for men like Mr. Dally afterwards."

Hilliard puzzled over this remark, and was on the point of making some impatient reply, but discretion restrained him. He turned to Eve's own affairs, questioned her closely about her life in the tradesman's house, and so their conversation followed a smoother course. Presently, half in jest, Hilliard mentioned Narramore's building projects.

"But who knows? It *might* come to something of importance for me. In two or three years, if all goes well, such a thing might possibly give me a start."

A singular solemnity had settled upon Eve's countenance. She spoke not a word, and seemed unaccountably ill at ease.

"Do you think I am in the clouds?" said Hilliard.

"Oh, no! Why shouldn't you get on—as other men do?"

But she would not dwell upon the hope, and Hilliard, not a little vexed, again became silent.

Her next visit was after a lapse of three weeks. She had again been suffering from a slight illness, and her pallor alarmed Hilliard. Again she began with talk of Patty Ringrose.

"Do you know, there's really a chance that we may see her before long! She'll have a holiday at Easter, from the Thursday night to Monday night, and I have all but got her to promise that she'll come over here. Wouldn't it be fun to let her see the Black Country? You remember her talk about it. I could get her a room, and if it's at all bearable weather, we would all have a day somewhere. Wouldn't you like that?"

"Yes; but I should greatly prefer a day with you alone."

"Oh, of course, the time is coming for that. Would you let us come here one day?"

With a persistence not to be mistaken Eve avoided all intimate topics; at the same time her manner grew more cordial. Through February and March, she decidedly improved in health. Hilliard saw her seldom, but she wrote frequent letters, and their note was as that of her conversation, lively, all but sportive. Once again she had become a mystery to her lover; he pondered over her very much as in the days when they were newly acquainted. Of one thing he felt but too well assured. She did not love him as he desired to be loved. Constant she might be, but is was the constancy of a woman unaffected with ardent emotion. If she granted him her lips they had no fervour respondent to his own; she made a sport of it, forgot it as soon as possible. Upon Hilliard's vehement nature this acted provocatively; at times he was all but frenzied with the violence of his sensual impulses. Yet Eve's control of him grew more assured the less she granted of herself; a look, a motion of her lips, and he drew apart, quivering but subdued. At one such moment he exclaimed;

"You had better not come here at all. I love you too insanely."

Eve looked at him, and silently began to shed tears. He implored her pardon, prostrated himself, behaved in a manner that justified his warning. But Eve stifled the serious drama of the situation, and forced him to laugh with her.

In these days architectural study made little way.

Patty Ringrose was coming for the Easter holidays. She would arrive on Good Friday. "As the weather is so very bad still," wrote Eve to Hilliard, "will you let us come to see you on Saturday? Sunday may be better for an excursion of some sort."

And thus it was arranged. Hilliard made ready his room to receive the fair visitors, who would come at about eleven in the morning. As usual nowadays, he felt discontented, but, after all, Patty's influence might be a help to him, as it had been in worse straits.


# CHAPTER XXI

To-day he had the house to himself. The corn-dealer's shop was closed, as on a Sunday; the optician and his blind wife had locked up their rooms and were spending Easter-tide, it might be hoped, amid more cheerful surroundings. Hilliard sat with his door open, that he might easily hear the knock which announced his guests at the entrance below.

It sounded, at length, but timidly. Had he not been listening, he would not have perceived it. Eve's handling of the knocker was firmer than that, and in a different rhythm. Apprehensive of disappointment, he hurried downstairs and opened the door to Patty Ringrose—Patty alone.

With a shy but pleased laugh, her cheeks warm and her eyes bright, she jerked out her hand to him as in the old days.

"I know you won't be glad to see me. I'm so sorry. I said I had better not come."

"Of course I am glad to see you. But where's Eve?"

"It's so unfortunate—she has such a bad headache!" panted the girl. "She couldn't possibly come, and I wanted to stay with her. I said I should only disappoint you."

"It's a pity, of course; but I'm glad you came, for all that." Hilliard stifled his dissatisfaction and misgivings. "You'll think this a queer sort of place. I'm quite alone here to-day. But after you have rested a little we can go somewhere else."

"Yes. Eve told me you would be so kind as to take me to see things. I'm not tired. I won't come in, if you'd rather——"

"Oh, you may as well see what sort of a den I've made for myself."

He led the way upstairs. When she reached the top, Patty was again breathless, the result of excitement more than exertion. She exclaimed at sight of the sitting-room. How cosy it was! What a scent from the flowers! Did he always buy flowers for his room? No doubt it was to please Eve. What a comfortable chair! Of course Eve always sat in this chair?

Then her babbling ceased, and she looked up at Hilliard, who stood over against her, with nervous delight. He could perceive no change whatever in her, except that she was better dressed than formerly. Not a day seemed to have been added to her age; her voice had precisely the intonations that he remembered. After all, it was little more than half a year since they were together in Paris; but to Hilliard the winter had seemed of interminable length, and he expected to find Miss Ringrose a much altered person.

"When did this headache begin?" he inquired, trying to speak without over-much concern.

"She had a little yesterday, when she met me at the station. I didn't think she was looking at all well."

"I'm surprised to hear that. She looked particularly well when I saw her last. Had you any trouble in making your way here?"

"Oh, not a bit. I found the tram, just as Eve told me. But I'm so sorry! And a fine day too! You don't often have fine days here, do you, Mr. Hilliard?"

"Now and then. So you've seen Dudley at last. What do you think of it?"

"Oh, I like it! I shouldn't mind living there a bit. But of course I like Birmingham better."

"Almost as fine as Paris, isn't it?"

"You don't mean that, of course. But I've only seen a few of the streets, and most of the shops are shut up to-day. Isn't it a pity Eve has to live so far off? Though, of course, it isn't really very far—and I suppose you see each other often?"

Hilliard took a seat, crossed his legs, and grasped his knee. The girl appeared to wait for an answer to her last words, but he said nothing, and stared at the floor.

"If it's fine to-morrow," Patty continued, after observing him furtively, "are you coming to Dudley?"

"Yes, I shall come over. Did she send any message?"

"No—nothing particular——"

Patty looked confused, stroked her dress, and gave a little cough.

"But if it rains—as it very likely will—there's no use in my coming."

"No, she said not."

"Or if her headache is still troubling her——"

"Let's hope it will be better. But—in any case, she'll be able to come with me to Birmingham on Monday, when I go back. I must be home again on Monday night."

"Don't you think," said Hilliard carelessly, "that Eve would rather have you to herself, just for the short time you are here?"

Patty made vigorous objection.

"I don't think that at all. It's quite settled that you are to come over to-morrow, if it's fine. Oh, and I *do* hope it will be! It would be so dreadful to be shut up in the house all day at Dudley. How very awkward that there's no place where she can have you there! If it rains, hadn't we better come here? I'm sure it would be better for Eve. She seems to get into such low spirits—just like she was sometimes in London."

"That's quite news to me," said the listener gravely.

"Doesn't she let you know? Then I'm so sorry I mentioned it. You won't tell her I said anything?"

"Wait a moment. Does she say that she is often in low spirits?"

Patty faltered, stroking her dress with the movement of increasing nervousness.

"It's better I should know," Hilliard added, "I'm afraid she keeps all this from me. For several weeks I have thought her in particularly good health."

"But she tells me just the opposite. She says——"

"Says what?"

"Perhaps it's only the place that doesn't agree with her. I don't think Dudley is *very* healthy, do you?"

"I never heard of doctors sending convalescents there. But Eve must be suffering from some other cause, I think. Does it strike you that she is at all like what she used to be when—when you felt so anxious about her?"

He met the girl's eyes, and saw them expand in alarm.

"I didn't think—I didn't mean——" she stammered.

"No, but I have a reason for asking. Is it so or not?"

"Don't frighten me, Mr. Hilliard! I do so wish I hadn't said anything. She isn't in good health, that's all. How can you think——? That was all over long ago. And she would never—I'm *sure* she wouldn't, after all you've done for her."

Hilliard ground the carpet with his foot, and all but uttered a violent ejaculation.

"I know she is all gratitude," were the words that became audible.

"She is indeed!" urged Patty. "She says that—even if she wished— she could never break off with you; as I am *sure* she would never wish!"

"Ah! that's what she says," murmured the other. And abruptly he rose. "There's no use in talking about this. You are here for a holiday, and not to be bored with other people's troubles. The sun is trying to shine. Let us go and see the town, and then—yes, I'll go back with you to Dudley, just to hear whether Eve is feeling any better. You could see her, and then come out and tell me."

"Mr. Hilliard, I'm quite sure you are worrying without any cause—you are, indeed!"

"I know I am. It's all nonsense. Come along, and let us enjoy the sunshine."

They spent three or four hours together, Hilliard resolute in his discharge of hospitable duties, and Miss Ringrose, after a brief spell of unnatural gravity, allowing no reflection to interfere with her holiday mood. Hilliard had never felt quite sure as to the limits of Patty's intelligence; he could not take her seriously, and yet felt unable to treat her altogether as a child or an imbecile. To-day, because of his preoccupied thoughts, and the effort it cost him to be jocose, he talked for the most part in a vein of irony which impressed, but did not much enlighten, his hearer.

"This," said he, when they had reached the centre of things, "is the Acropolis of Birmingham. Here are our great buildings, of which we boast to the world. They signify the triumph of Democracy—and of money. In front of you stands the Town Hall. Here, to the left, is the Midland Institute, where a great deal of lecturing goes on, and the big free library, where you can either read or go to sleep. I have done both in my time. Behind yonder you catch a glimpse of the fountain that plays to the glory of Joseph Chamberlain—did you ever hear of him? And further back still is Mason College, where young men are taught a variety of things, including discontent with a small income. To the right there, that's the Council Hall—splendid, isn't it! We bring our little boys to look at it, and tell them if they make money enough they may some day go in and out as if it were their own house. Behind it you see the Art Gallery. We don't really care for pictures; a great big machine is our genuine delight; but it wouldn't be nice to tell everybody that."

"What a lot I have learnt from you!" exclaimed the girl ingenuously, when at length they turned their steps towards the railway station. "I shall always remember Birmingham. You like it much better than London, don't you?"

"I glory in the place!"

Hilliard was tired out. He repented of his proposal to make the journey to Dudley and back, but his companion did not suspect this.

"I'm sure Eve will come out and have a little walk with us," she said comfortingly. "And she'll think it so kind of you."

At Dudley station there were crowds of people; Patty asked leave to hold by her companion's arm as they made their way to the exit. Just outside Hilliard heard himself hailed in a familiar voice; he turned and saw Narramore.

"I beg your pardon," said his friend, coming near. "I didn't notice—I thought you were alone, or, of course I shouldn't have shouted. Shall you be at home to-morrow afternoon?"

"If it rains."

"It's sure to rain. I shall look in about four."

## CHAPTER XXII

With a glance at Miss Ringrose, he raised his hat and passed on. Hilliard, confused by the rapid rencontre, half annoyed at having been seen with Patty, and half wishing he had not granted the appointment for to-morrow, as it might interfere with a visit from the girls, walked forward in silence.

"So we really sha'n't see you if it's wet to-morrow," said Patty.

"Better not. Eve would be afraid to come, she catches cold so easily."

"It may be fine, like to-day. I do hope——"

She broke off and added:

"Why, isn't that Eve in front?"

Eve it certainly was, walking slowly away from the station, a few yards in advance of them. They quickened their pace, and Patty caught her friend by the arm. Eve, startled out of abstraction, stared at her with eyes of dismay and bloodless cheeks.

"Did I frighten you? Mr. Hilliard has come back with me to ask how you are. Is your head better?"

"I've just been down to the station—for something to do," said Eve, her look fixed on Hilliard with what seemed to him a very strange intensity. "The afternoon was so fine."

"We've had a splendid time," cried Patty. "Mr. Hilliard has shown me everything."

"I'm so glad. I should only have spoilt it if I had been with you. It's wretched going about with a headache, and I can't make believe to enjoy Birmingham."

Eve spoke hurriedly, still regarding Hilliard, who looked upon the ground.

"Have you been alone all day?" he asked, taking the outer place at her side, as they walked on.

"Of course—except for the people in the house," was her offhand reply.

"I met Narramore down at the station; he must have passed you. What has brought him here to-day, I wonder?"

Appearing not to heed the remark, Eve glanced across at Patty, and said with a laugh:

"It's like Paris again, isn't it—we three? You ought to come and live here, Patty. Don't you think you could get a place in Birmingham? Mr. Hilliard would get a piano for his room, and you could let him have some music. I'm too old to learn."

"I'm sure he wouldn't want *me* jingling there."

"Wouldn't he? He's very fond of music indeed."

Hilliard stopped.

"Well, I don't think I'll go any further," he said mechanically. "You're quite well again, Eve, and that's all I wanted to know."

"What about to-morrow?" Eve asked.

The sun had set, and in the westward sky rose a mountain of menacing cloud. Hilliard gave a glance in that direction before replying.

"Don't count upon me. Patty and you will enjoy the day together, in any case. Yes, I had rather have it so. Narramore said just now he might look in to see me in the afternoon. But come over on Monday. When does Patty's train go from New Street?"

Eve was mute, gazing at the speaker as if she did not catch what he had said. Patty answered for herself.

"Then you can either come to my place," he continued, "or I'll meet you at the station."

Patty's desire was evident in her face; she looked at Eve.

"We'll come to you early in the afternoon," said the latter, speaking like one aroused from reverie. "Yes, we'll come whatever the weather is."

The young man shook hands with them, raised his hat, and walked

away without further speech. It occurred to him that he might
overtake Narramore at the station, and in that hope he hastened; but
Narramore must have left by a London and North-Western train
which had just started; he was nowhere discoverable. Hilliard
travelled back by the Great Western, after waiting about an hour; he
had for companions half-a-dozen beer-muddled lads, who roared
hymns and costers' catches impartially.

His mind was haunted with deadly suspicions: he felt sick at heart.

Eve's headache, undoubtedly, was a mere pretence for not
accompanying Patty to-day. She had desired to be alone, and—this he
discovered no less clearly—she wished the friendship between him and
Patty to be fostered. With what foolish hope? Was she so shallow-
natured as to imagine that he might transfer his affections to Patty
Ringrose? It proved how strong her desire had grown to be free from
him.

The innocent Patty (*was* she so innocent?) seemed not to suspect the
meaning of her friend's talk. Yet Eve must have all but told her in so
many words that she was weary of her lover. That hateful harping on
"gratitude"! Well, one cannot purchase a woman's love. He had
missed the right, the generous, line of conduct. That would have been
to rescue Eve from manifest peril, and then to ask nothing of her.
Could he but have held his passions in leash, something like friendship—rarest of all relations between man and woman—might have
come about between him and Eve. She, too, certainly had never got
beyond the stage of liking him as a companion; her senses had never
answered to his appeal. He looked back upon the evening when they
had dined together at the restaurant in Holborn. Could he but have
stopped at *that* point! There would have been no harm in such
avowals as then escaped him, for he recognised without bitterness that
the warmth of feeling was all on one side, and Eve, in the manner of
her sex, could like him better for his love without a dream of returning
it. His error was to have taken advantage—perhaps a mean
advantage—of the strange events that followed. If he restrained
himself before, how much more he should have done so when the girl
had put herself at his mercy, when to demand her love was the
obvious, commonplace, vulgar outcome of the situation? Of course she
harped on "gratitude." What but a sense of obligation had
constrained her?

Something had taken place to-day; he felt it as a miserable
certainty. The man from London had been with her. She expected
him, and had elaborately planned for a day of freedom. Perhaps her
invitation of Patty had no other motive.

That Patty was a conspirator against him he could not believe. No!
She was merely an instrument of Eve's subtlety. And his suspicion had

not gone beyond the truth. Eve entertained the hope that Patty might take her place. Perchance the silly, good-natured girl would feel no objection; though it was not very likely that she foresaw or schemed for such an issue.

At Snow Hill station it cost him an effort to rise and leave the carriage. His mood was sluggish; he wished to sit still and think idly over the course of events.

He went by way of St. Philip's Church, which stands amid a wide graveyard, enclosed with iron railings, and crossed by paved walks. The locality was all but forsaken; the church rose black against the grey sky, and the lofty places of business round about were darkly silent. A man's footstep sounded in front of him, and a figure approached along the narrow path between the high bars. Hilliard would have passed without attention, but the man stopped his way.

"Hollo! Here we are again!"

He stared at the speaker, and recognised Mr. Dengate.

"So you've come back?"

"Where from?" said Hilliard. "What do you know of me?"

"As much as I care to," replied the other with a laugh. "So you haven't quite gone to the devil yet? I gave you six months. I've been watching the police news in the London papers."

In a maddening access of rage, Hilliard clenched his fist and struck fiercely at the man. But he did no harm, for his aim was wild, and Dengate easily warded off the blows.

"Hold on! You're drunk, of course. Stop it, my lad, or I'll have you locked up till Monday morning. Very obliging of you to offer me the pleasure I was expecting, but you *will* have it, eh?"

A second blow was repaid in kind, and Hilliard staggered back against the railings. Before he could recover himself, Dengate, whose high hat rolled between their feet, pinned his arms.

"There's someone coming along. It's a pity. I should enjoy thrashing you and then running you in. But a man of my position doesn't care to get mixed up in a street row. It wouldn't sound well at Liverpool. Stand quiet, will you!"

A man and a woman drew near, and lingered for a moment in curiosity. Hilliard already amazed at what he had done, became passive, and stood with bent head.

"I must have a word or two with you," said Dengate, when he had picked up his hat. "Can you walk straight? I didn't notice you were drunk before I spoke to you. Come along this way."

To escape the lookers-on, Hilliard moved forward.

"I've always regretted," resumed his companion, "that I didn't give you a sound thrashing that night in the train. It would have done you good. It might have been the making of you. I didn't hurt you, eh?"

"You've bruised my lips—that's all. And I deserved it for being such a damned fool as to lose my temper."

"You look rather more decent than I should have expected. What have you been doing in London?"

"How do you know I have been in London?"

"I took that for granted when I knew you'd left your work at Dudley."

"Who told you I had left it?"

"What does it matter?"

"I should like to know," said Hilliard, whose excitement had passed and left him cold. "And I should like to know who told you before that I was in the habit of getting drunk?"

"Are you drunk now, or not?"

"Not in the way you mean. Do you happen to know a man called Narramore?"

"Never heard the name."

Hilliard felt ashamed of his ignoble suspicion. He became silent.

"There's no reason why you shouldn't be told," added Dengate; "it was a friend of yours at Dudley that I came across when I was making inquiries about you: Mullen his name was."

A clerk at the ironworks, with whom Hilliard had been on terms of slight intimacy.

"Oh, that fellow," he uttered carelessly. "I'm glad to know it was no one else. Why did you go inquiring about me?"

"I told you. If I'd heard a better account I should have done a good deal more for you than pay that money. I gave you a chance, too. If you'd shown any kind of decent behaviour when I spoke to you in the train—but it's no good talking about that now. This is the second time you've let me see what a natural blackguard you are. It's queer, too; you didn't get that from your father. I could have put you in the way of something good at Liverpool. Now, I'd see you damned first. Well, have you run through the money?"

"Every penny of it gone in drink."

"And what are you doing?"

"Walking with a man I should be glad to be rid of."

"All right. Here's my card. When you get into the gutter, and nobody'll give you a hand out, let me know."

With a nod, Dengate walked off. Hilliard saw him smoothe his silk hat as he went; then, without glancing at the card, he threw it away.

The next morning was cold and wet. He lay in bed till eleven o'clock, when the char-woman came to put his rooms in order. At mid-day he left home, had dinner at the nearest place he knew where a meal could be obtained on Sunday, and afterwards walked the streets for an hour under his umbrella. The exercise did him good; on

returning he felt able to sit down by the fire, and turn over the plates
of his great book on French Cathedrals. This, at all events, remained
to him out of the wreck, and was a joy that could be counted upon in
days to come.

He hoped Narramore would keep his promise, and was not disappointed. On the verge of dusk his friend knocked and entered.

"The blind woman was at the door below," he explained, "looking
for somebody."

"It isn't as absurd as it sounds. She does look for people—with her
ears. She knows a footstep that no one else can hear. What were you
doing at Dudley yesterday?"

Narramore took his pipe out of its case and smiled over it.

"Colours well, doesn't it?" he remarked. "You don't care about the
colouring of a pipe? I get a lot of satisfaction out of such little things!
Lazy fellows always do; and they have the best of life in the end. By-
the-bye, what were *you* doing at Dudley?"

"Had to go over with a girl."

"Rather a pretty girl, too. Old acquaintance?"

"Someone I got to know in London. No, no, not at all what you
suppose."

"Well, I know you wouldn't talk about it. It isn't my way; either,
to say much about such things. But I half-promised, not long ago, to
let you know of something that was going on—if it came to anything.
And it rather looks as if it might. What do you think! Birching has
been at me, wanting to know why I don't call. I wonder whether the
girl put him up to it?"

"You went rather far, didn't you?"

"Oh, I drew back in time. Besides, those ideas are old-fashioned.
It'll have to be understood that marriageable girls have nothing specially sacred about them. They must associate with men on equal
terms. The day has gone by for a hulking brother to come asking a
man about his 'intentions.' As a rule, it's the girl that has intentions.
The man is just looking round, anxious to be amiable without making
a fool of himself. We're at a great disadvantage. A girl who isn't an
idiot can very soon know all about the men who interest her; but it's
devilish difficult to get much insight into *them*—until you've hopelessly committed yourself—won't you smoke? I've something to tell
you, and I can't talk to a man who isn't smoking, when my own pipe's
lit."

Hilliard obeyed, and for a few moments they puffed in silence, twi-
light thickening about them.

"Three or four months ago," resumed Narramore, "I was told one
day—at business—that a lady wished to see me. I happened to have
the room to myself, and told them to show the lady in. I didn't in the

least know who it could be, and I was surprised to see rather a good-looking girl—not exactly a lady—tallish, and with fine dark eyes—what did you say?"

"Nothing."

"A twinge of gout?"

"Go on."

Narramore scrutinised his friend, who spoke in an unusual tone.

"She sat down, and began to tell me that she was out of work—wanted a place as a bookkeeper, or something of the kind. Could I help her? I asked her why she came to *me*. She said she had heard of me from someone who used to be employed at our place. That was flattering. I showed my sense of it. Then I asked her name, and she said it was Miss Madeley."

A gust threw rain against the windows. Narramore paused, looking into the fire, and smiling thoughtfully.

# CHAPTER XXIII

"You foresee the course of the narrative?"

"Better tell it in detail," muttered Hilliard.

"Why this severe tone? Do you anticipate something that will shock your moral sense? I didn't think you were so straitlaced."

"Do you mean to say——"

Hilliard was sitting upright; his voice began on a harsh tremor, and suddenly failed. The other gazed at him in humorous astonishment.

"What the devil do you mean? Even suppose—who made you a judge and a ruler? This is the most comical start I've known for a long time. I was going to tell you that I have made up my mind to marry the girl."

"I see—it's all right——"

"But do you really mean," said Narramore, "that anything else would have aroused your moral indignation?"

Hilliard burst into a violent fit of laughter. His pipe fell to the floor, and broke; whereupon he interrupted his strange merriment with a savage oath.

"It was a joke, then?" remarked his friend.

"Your monstrous dulness shows the state of your mind. This is what comes of getting entangled with women. You need to have a sense of humour."

"I'm afraid there's some truth in what you say, old boy. I've been conscious of queer symptoms lately—a disposition to take things with absurd seriousness, and an unwholesome bodily activity now and then."

"Go on with your tragic story. The girl asked you to find her a place——"

"I promised to think about it, but I couldn't hear of anything suitable. She had left her address with me, so at length I wrote her a line just saying I hadn't forgotten her. I got an answer on black-edged paper. Miss Madeley wrote to tell me that her father had recently died, and that she had found employment at Dudley; with thanks for my kindness—and so on. It was rather a nicely written letter, and after a day or two I wrote again. I heard nothing—hardly expected to; so in a fort-night's time I wrote once more. Significant, wasn't it? I'm not fond of writing letters, as you know. But I've written a good many since then. At last it came to another meeting. I went over to Dudley on purpose, and saw Miss Madeley on the Castle Hill. I had liked the look of her from the first, and I liked it still better now. By dint of persuasion, I made her tell me all about herself."

"Did she tell you the truth?"

"Why should you suppose she didn't?" replied Narramore with some emphasis. "You must look at this affair in a different light, Hilliard. A joke is a joke, but I've told you that the joking time has gone by. I can make allowance for you: you think I have been making a fool of myself, after all."

"The beginning was ominous."

"The beginning of our acquaintance? Yes, I know how it strikes you. But she came in that way because she had been trying for months——"

"Who was it that told her of you?"

"Oh, one of our girls, no doubt. I haven't asked her—never thought again about it."

"And what's her record?"

"Nothing dramatic in it, I'm glad to say. At one time she had an engagement in London for a year or two. Her people, 'poor but honest'—as the stories put it. Father was a timekeeper at Dudley; brother, a mechanic there. I was over to see her yesterday; we had only just said good-bye when I met you. She's remarkably well educated, all things considered: very fond of reading; knows as much of books as I do—more, I daresay. First-rate intelligence; I guessed that from the first. I can see the drawbacks, of course. As I said, she isn't what *you* would call a lady; but there's nothing much to find fault with even in her manners. And the long and the short of it is, I'm in love with her."

"And she has promised to marry you?"

"Well, not in so many words. She seems to have scruples—difference of position, and that kind of thing."

"Very reasonable scruples, no doubt."

"Quite right that she should think of it in that way, at all events. But I believe it was practically settled yesterday. She isn't in very brilliant health, poor girl! I want to get her away from that beastly place as soon as possible. I shall give myself a longish holiday, and take her on to the Continent. A thorough change of that kind would set her up wonderfully."

"She has never been on to the Continent?"

"What a preposterous question! You're going to sleep, sitting here in the dark. Oh, don't trouble to light up for me; I can't stay much longer."

Hilliard had risen, but instead of lighting the lamp he turned to the window and stood there drumming with his fingers on a pane.

"Are you seriously concerned for me?" said his friend. "Does it seem a piece of madness?"

"You must judge for yourself, Narramore."

"When you have seen her I think you'll take my views. Of course it's the very last thing I ever imagined myself doing; but I begin to see that the talk about fate isn't altogether humbug. I want this girl for my wife, and I never met any one else whom I really *did* want. She suits me exactly. It isn't as if I thought of marrying an ordinary, ignorant, low-class girl. Eve—that's her name—is very much out of the common, look at her how you may. She's rather melancholy, but that's a natural result of her life."

"No doubt, as you say, she wants a thorough change," remarked Hilliard, smiling in the gloom.

"That's it. Her nerves are out of order. Well, I thought I should like to tell you this, old chap. You'll get over the shock in time. I more than half believe, still, that your moral indignation was genuine. And why not? I ought to respect you for it."

"Are you going?"

"I must be in Bristol Road by five—promised to drink a cup of Mrs. Stocker's tea this afternoon. I'm glad now that I have kept up a few homely acquaintances; they may be useful. Of course I shall throw over the Birchings and that lot. You see now why my thoughts have been running on a country house!"

He went off laughing, and his friend sat down again by the fireside.

Half an hour passed. The fire had burnt low, and the room was quite dark. At length, Hilliard bestirred himself. He lit the lamp, drew down the blind, and seated himself at the table to write. With great rapidity he covered four sides of note-paper, and addressed an envelope. But he had no postage-stamp. It could be obtained at a tobacconist's.

So he went out, and turned towards a little shop hard by. But when he had stamped the letter he felt undecided about posting it. Eve had promised to come to-morrow with Patty. If she again failed him it would be time enough to write. If she kept her promise the presence of a third person would be an intolerable restraint upon him. Yet why? Patty might as well know all, and act as judge between them. There needed little sagacity to arbitrate in a matter such as this.

To sit at home was impossible. He walked for the sake of walking, straight on, without object. Down the long gas-lit perspective of Bradford Street, with its closed, silent work-shops, across the miserable little river Rea—canal rather than river, sewer rather than canal—up the steep ascent to St. Martin's and the Bull Ring, and the bronze Nelson, dripping with dirty moisture; between the big buildings of New Street, and so to the centre of the town. At the corner by the Post Office he stood in idle contemplation. Rain was still falling, but lightly. The great open space gleamed with shafts of yellow radiance reflected on wet asphalt from the numerous lamps. There was little traffic. An omnibus clattered by, and a tottery cab, both looking rain-soaked. Near the statue of Peel stood a hansom, the forlorn horse crooking his knees and hanging his hopeless head. The Town Hall colonnade sheltered a crowd of people, who were waiting for the rain to stop, that they might spend their Sunday evening, as usual, in rambling about the streets. Within the building, which showed light through all its long windows, a religious meeting was in progress, and hundreds of voices peeled forth a rousing hymn, fortified with deeper organ-note.

Hilliard noticed that as rain-drops fell on the heated globes of the street-lamps they were thrown off again in little jets and puffs of steam. This phenomenon amused him for several minutes. He wondered that he had never observed it before.

Easter Sunday. The day had its importance for a Christian mind. Did Eve think about that? Perhaps her association with him, careless as he was in all such matters, had helped to blunt her religious feeling. Yet what hope was there, in such a world as this, that she would retain the pieties of her girlhood?

Easter Sunday. As he walked on, he pondered the Christian story, and tried to make something out of it. Had it any significance for *him?* Perhaps, for he had never consciously discarded the old faith; he had simply let it fall out of his mind. But a woman ought to have religious convictions. Yes; he saw the necessity of that. Better for him if Eve were in the Town Hall yonder, joining her voice with those that sang.

Better for *him.* A selfish point of view. But the advantage would be hers also. Did he not desire her happiness? He tried to think so, but after all was ashamed to play the sophist with himself. The letter he carried in his pocket told the truth. He had but to think of her as mar-

ried to Robert Narramore and the jealous fury of natural man drove
him headlong.

Monday was again a holiday. When would the cursed people get
back to their toil, and let the world resume its wonted grind and
clang? They seemed to have been making holiday for a month past.

He walked up and down on the pavement near his door, until at the
street corner there appeared a figure he knew. It was Patty Ringrose,
again unaccompanied.

# CHAPTER XXIV

They shook hands without a word, their eyes meeting for an instant
only. Hilliard led the way upstairs; and Patty, still keeping an embarrassed silence, sat down on the easy-chair. Her complexion was as
noticeably fresh as Hilliard's was wan and fatigued. Where Patty's
skin showed a dimple, his bore a gash, the result of an accident in
shaving this morning.

With hands behind he stood in front of the girl.

"She chose not to come, then?"

"Yes. She asked me to come and see you alone."

"No pretence of headache this time."

"I don't think it was a pretence," faltered Patty, who looked very ill
at ease, for all the bloom on her cheeks and the clear, childish light in
her eyes.

"Well, then, why hasn't she come to-day?"

"She has sent a letter for you, Mr. Hilliard."

Patty handed the missive, and Hilliard laid it upon the table.

"Am I to read it now?"

"I think it's a long letter."

"Feels like it. I'll study it at my leisure. You know what it
contains?"

Patty nodded, her face turned away.

"And why has she chosen to-day to write to me?" Patty kept
silence. "Anything to do with the call I had yesterday from my friend
Narramore?"

"Yes—that's the reason. But she has meant to let you know for
some time."

Hilliard drew a long breath. He fixed his eyes on the letter.

"She has told me everything," the girl continued, speaking hurriedly. "Did you know about it before yesterday?"

"I'm not so good an actor as all that. Eve has the advantage of me in that respect. She really thought it possible that Narramore had spoken before?"

"She couldn't be sure."

"H'm! Then she didn't know for certain that Narramore was going to talk to me about her yesterday?"

"She knew it *must* come."

"Patty, our friend Miss Madeley is a very sensible person—don't you think so?"

"You mustn't think she made a plan to deceive you. She tells you all about it in the letter, and I'm quite sure it's all true, Mr. Hilliard. I was astonished when I heard of it, and I can't tell you how sorry I feel——"

"I'm not at all sure that there's any cause for sorrow," Hilliard interrupted, drawing up a chair and throwing himself upon it. "Unless you mean that you are sorry for Eve."

"I meant that as well."

"Let us understand each other. How much has she told you?"

"Everything, from beginning to end. I had no idea of what happened in London before we went to Paris. And she does so repent of it! She doesn't know how she could do it. She wishes you had refused her."

"So do I."

"But you saved her—she can never forget that. You musn't think that she only pretends to be grateful. She will be grateful to you as long as she lives. I know she will."

"On condition that I—what?"

Patty gave him a bewildered look.

"What does she ask of me now?"

"She's ashamed to ask anything. She fears you will never speak to her again."

Hilliard meditated, then glanced at the letter.

"I had better read this now, I think, if you will let me."

"Yes—please do——"

He tore open the envelope, and disclosed two sheets of note-paper, covered with writing. For several minutes there was silence; Patty now and then gave a furtive glance at her companion's face as he was reading. At length he put the letter down again, softly.

"There's something more here than I expected. Can you tell me whether she heard from Narramore this morning?"

"She has had no letter."

"I see. And what does she suppose passed between Narramore and me yesterday?"

"She is wondering what you told him."

"She takes it for granted, in this letter, that I have put an end to everything between them. Well, hadn't I a right to do so?"

"Of course you had," Patty replied, with emphasis. "And she knew it must come. She never really thought that she could marry Mr. Narramore. She gave him no promise."

"Only corresponded with him, and made appointments with him, and allowed him to feel sure that she would be his wife."

"Eve has behaved very strangely. I can't understand her. She ought to have told you that she had been to see him, and that he wrote to her. It's always best to be straightforward. See what trouble she has got herself into!"

Hilliard took up the letter again, and again there was a long silence.

"Have you said good-bye to her?" were his next words.

"She's going to meet me at the station to see me off."

"Did she come from Dudley with you?"

"No."

"It's all very well to make use of you for this disagreeable business——"

"Oh, I didn't mind it!" broke in Patty, with irrelevant cheerfulness.

"A woman who does such things as this should have the courage to go through with it. She ought to have come herself, and have told me that. She was aiming at much better things than *I* could have promised her. There would have been something to admire in that. The worst of it is she is making me feel ashamed of her. I'd rather have to do with a woman who didn't care a rap for my feelings than with a weak one, who tried to spare me to advantage herself at the same time. There's nothing like courage, whether in good or evil. What do you think? Does she like Narramore?"

"I think she does," faltered Patty, nervously striking her dress.

"Is she in love with him?"

"I—I really don't know!"

"Do you think she ever was in love with anyone, or ever will be?"

Patty sat mute.

"Just tell me what you think."

"I'm afraid she never—Oh, I don't like to say it, Mr. Hilliard!"

"That she never was in love with *me?* I know it."

His tone caused Patty to look up at him, and what she saw in his face made her say quickly:

"I am so sorry; I am indeed! You deserve——"

"Never mind what I deserve," Hilliard interrupted with a grim smile. "Something less than hanging, I hope. That fellow in London; she was fond of *him?*"

The girl whispered an assent.

"A pity I interfered."

"Ah! But think what——"

"We won't discuss it, Patty. It's a horrible thing to be mad about a girl who cares no more for you than for an old glove; but it's a fool's part to try to win her by the way of gratitude. When we came back from Paris I ought to have gone my way, and left her to go hers. Perhaps just possible—if I had seemed to think no more of her——"

Patty waited, but he did not finish his speech.

"What are you going to do, Mr. Hilliard?"

"Yes, that's the question. Shall I hold her to her promise? She says here that she will keep her word if I demand it."

"She says that!" Patty exclaimed, with startled eyes.

"Didn't you know?"

"She told me it was impossible. But perhaps she didn't mean it. Who can tell *what* she means?"

For the first time there sounded a petulance in the girl's voice. Her lips closed tightly, and she tapped with her foot on the floor.

"Did she say that the other thing was also impossible—to marry Narramore?"

"She thinks it is, after what you've told him."

"Well, now, as a matter of fact I told him nothing."

Patty stared, a new light in her eyes.

"You told him—nothing?"

"I just let him suppose that I had never heard the girl's name before."

"Oh, how kind of you! How——"

"Please to remember that it wasn't very easy to tell the truth. What sort of figure should I have made?"

"It's too bad of Eve! It's cruel! I can never like her as I did before."

"Oh, she's very interesting. She gives one such a lot to talk about."

"I don't like her, and I shall tell her so before I leave Birmingham. What right has she to make people so miserable?"

"Only one, after all."

"Do you mean that you will let her marry Mr. Narramore?" Patty asked with interest.

"We shall have to talk about that."

"If I were you I should never see her again!"

"The probability is that we shall see each other many a time."

"Then *you* haven't much courage, Mr. Hilliard!" exclaimed the girl, with a flush on her cheeks.

"More than you think, perhaps," he answered between his teeth.

"Men are very strange," Patty commented in a low voice of scorn, mitigated by timidity.

"Yes, we play queer pranks when a woman has made a slave of us. I suppose you think I should have too much pride to care any more for her. The truth is that for years to come I shall tremble all through whenever she is near me. Such love as I have felt for Eve won't be trampled out like a spark. It's the best and the worst part of my life. No woman can ever be to me what Eve is."

Abashed by the grave force of this utterance, Patty shrank back into the chair, and held her peace.

"You will very soon know what comes of it all," Hilliard continued with a sudden change of voice. "It has to be decided pretty quickly, one way or another."

"May I tell Eve what you have said to me?" the girl asked with diffidence.

"Yes, anything that I have said."

Patty lingered a little, then, as her companion said no more, she rose.

"I must say good-bye, Mr. Hilliard."

"I am afraid your holiday hasn't been as pleasant as you expected."

"Oh, I have enjoyed myself very much. And I hope"—her voice wavered—"I do hope it'll be all right. I'm sure you'll do what seems best."

"I shall do what I find myself obliged to, Patty. Good-bye. I won't offer to go with you, for I should be poor company."

He conducted her to the foot of the stairs, again shook hands with her, put all his good-will into a smile, and watched her trip away with a step not so light as usual. Then he returned to Eve's letter. It gave him a detailed account of her relations with Narramore. "I went to him because I couldn't bear to live idle any longer; I had no other thought in my mind. If he had been the means of my finding work, I should have confessed it to you at once. But I was tempted into answering his letters. . . . I knew I was behaving wrongly; I can't defend myself. . . . I have never concealed my faults from you—the greatest of them is my fear of poverty. I believe it is this that has prevented me from returning your love as I wished to do. For a long time I have been playing a deceitful part, and the strange thing is that I *knew* my exposure might come at any moment. I seem to have been led on by a sort of despair. Now I am tired of it; whether you were prepared for this or not, I must tell you. . . . I don't ask you to release me. I have been wronging you and acting against my conscience, and if you can forgive me I will try to make up for the ill I have done. . . ."

How much of this could he believe? Gladly he would have fooled himself into believing it all, but the rational soul in him cast out credulity. Every phrase of the letter was calculated for its impression.

And the very risk she had run, was not that too a matter of deliberate speculation? She *might* succeed in her design upon Narramore; if she failed, the poorer man was still to be counted upon, for she knew the extent of her power over him. It was worth the endeavour. Perhaps, in her insolent self-confidence, she did not fear the effect on Narramore of the disclosure that might be made to him. And who could say that her boldness was not likely to be justified?

He burned with wrath against her, the wrath of a hopelessly infatuated man. Thoughts of revenge, no matter how ignoble, harassed his mind. She counted on his slavish spirit, and even in saying that she did not ask him to release her, she saw herself already released. At each reperusal of her letter he felt more resolved to disappoint the hope that inspired it. When she learnt from Patty that Narramore was still ignorant of her history, how would she exult! But that joy should be brief. In the name of common honesty he would protect his friend. If Narramore chose to take her with his eyes open——

Jealous frenzy kept him pacing the room for an hour or two. Then he went forth and haunted the neighbourhood of New Street station until within five minutes of the time of departure of Patty's train. If Eve kept her promise to see the girl off he might surprise her upon the platform.

From the bridge crossing the lines he surveyed the crowd of people that waited by the London train, a bank-holiday train taking back a freight of excursionists. There-amid he discovered Eve, noted her position, descended to the platform, and got as near to her as possible. The train moved off. As Eve turned away among the dispersing people, he stepped to meet her.

# CHAPTER XXV

She gave no sign of surprise. Hilliard read in her face that she had prepared herself for this encounter.

"Come away where we can talk," he said abruptly.

She walked by him to a part of the station where only a porter passed occasionally. The echoings beneath the vaulted roof allowed them to speak without constraint, for their voices were inaudible a yard or two off. Hilliard would not look into her face, lest he should be softened to foolish clemency.

"It's very kind of you," he began, with no clear purpose save the desire of harsh speech, "to ask me to overlook this trifle, and let things be as before."

"I have said all I *can* say in the letter. I deserve all your anger."

That was the note he dreaded, the too well remembered note of pathetic submission. It reminded him with intolerable force that he had never held her by any bond save that of her gratitude.

"Do you really imagine," he exclaimed, "that I could go on with make-believe—that I could bring myself to put faith in you again for a moment?"

"I don't ask you to," Eve replied, in firmer accents. "I have lost what little respect you could ever feel for me. I might have repaid you with honesty—I didn't do even that. Say the worst you can of me, and I shall think still worse of myself."

The voice overcame him with a conviction of her sincerity, and he gazed at her, marvelling.

"Are you honest *now?* Anyone would think so; yet how am I to believe it?"

Eve met his eyes steadily.

"I will never again say one word to you that isn't pure truth. I am at your mercy, and you may punish me as you like."

"There's only one way in which I can punish you. For the loss of *my* respect, or of my love, you care nothing. If I bring myself to tell Narramore disagreeable things about you, you will suffer a disappointment, and that's all. The cost to me will be much greater, and you know it. You pity yourself. You regard me as holding you ungenerously by an advantage you once gave me. It isn't so at all. It is I who have been held by bonds I couldn't break, and from the day when you pretended a love you never felt, all the blame lay with you."

"What could I do?"

"Be truthful—that was all."

"You were not content with the truth. You forced me to think that I could love you. Only remember what passed between us."

"Honesty was still possible, when you came to know yourself better. You should have said to me in so many words: 'I can't look forward to our future with any courage; if I marry it must be a man who has more to offer.' Do you think I couldn't have endured to hear that? You have never understood me. I should have said: 'Then let us shake hands, and I am your friend to help you all I can.'"

"You say that *now*——"

"I should have said it at any time."

"But I am not so mean as you think me. If I loved a man I could face poverty with him, much as I hate and dread it. It was because I only liked you, and could not feel more——"

"Your love happens to fall upon a man who has solid possessions."

"It's easy to speak so scornfully. I have not pretended to love the man you mean."

"Yet you have brought him to think that you are willing to marry him."

"Without any word of love from me. If I had been free I would have married him—just because I am sick of the life I lead, and long for the kind of life he offered me."

"When it's too late you are frank enough."

"Despise me as much as you like. You want the truth, and you shall hear nothing else from me."

"Well, we get near to understanding each other. But it astonishes me that you spoilt your excellent chance. How could you hope to carry through this——?"

Eve broke in impatiently.

"I told you in the letter that I had no hope of it. It's your mistake to think me a crafty, plotting, selfish woman. I'm only a very miserable one—it went on from this to that, and I meant nothing. I didn't scheme; I was only tempted into foolishness. I felt myself getting into difficulties that would be my ruin, but I hadn't strength to draw back."

"You do yourself injustice," said Hilliard, coldly. "For the past month you have acted a part before me, and acted it well. You seemed to be reconciling yourself to my prospects, indifferent as they were. You encouraged me—talked with unusual cheerfulness—showed a bright face. If this wasn't deliberate acting what did it mean?"

"Yes, it was put on," Eve admitted, after a pause. "But I couldn't help that. I was obliged to keep seeing you, and if I had looked as miserable as I felt——" She broke off. "I tried to behave just like a friend. You can't charge me with pretending—anything else. I *could* be your friend: that was honest feeling."

"It's no use to me. I must have more, or nothing."

The flood of passion surged in him again. Some trick of her voice, or some indescribable movement of her head—the trifles which are all-powerful over a man in love—beat down his contending reason.

"You say," he continued, "that you will make amends for your unfair dealing. If you mean it, take the only course that shows itself. Confess to Narramore what you have done; you owe it to him as much as to me."

"I can't do that," said Eve, drawing away. "It's for you to tell him—if you like."

"No. I had my opportunity, and let it pass. I don't mean that you are to inform him of all there has been between us; that's needless. We have agreed to forget everything that suggests the word I hate. But that you and I have been lovers and looked—I, at all events—to be something more, this you must let him know."

"I can never do that."

"Without it, how are you to disentangle yourself?"

"I promise you he shall see no more of me."

"Such a promise is idle, and you know it. Remember, too, that Narramore and I are friends. He will speak to me of you, and I can't play a farce with him. It would be intolerable discomfort to me, and grossly unfair to him. Do, for once, the simple, honourable thing, and make a new beginning. After that, be guided by your own interests. Assuredly I shall not stand in your way."

Eve had turned her eyes in the direction of crowd and bustle. When she faced Hilliard again, he saw that she had come to a resolve.

"There's only one way out of it for me," she said impulsively. "I can't talk any longer. I'll write to you."

She moved from him; Hilliard followed. At a distance of half-a-dozen yards, just as he was about to address her again, she stopped and spoke——

"You hate to hear me talk of 'gratitude.' I have always meant by it less than you thought. I was grateful for the money, not for anything else. When you took me away, perhaps it was the unkindest thing you could have done."

An unwonted vehemence shook her voice. Her muscles were tense; she stood in an attitude of rebellious pride.

"If I had been true to myself then—— But it isn't too late. If I am to act honestly, I know very well what I must do. I will take your advice."

Hilliard could not doubt of her meaning. He remembered his last talk with Patty. This was a declaration he had not foreseen, and it affected him otherwise than he could have anticipated.

"My advice had nothing to do with *that*," was his answer, as he read her face. "But I shall say not a word against it. I could respect you, at all events."

"Yes, and I had rather have your respect than your love."

With that, she left him. He wished to pursue, but a physical languor held him motionless. And when at length he sauntered from the place, it was with a sense of satisfaction at what had happened. Let her carry out that purpose: he faced it, preferred it. Let her be lost to him in that way rather than any other. It cut the knot, and left him with a memory of Eve that would not efface her dishonouring weakness.

Late at night, he walked about the streets near his home, debating with himself whether she would act as she spoke, or had only sought to frighten him with a threat. And still he hoped that her resolve was sincere. He could bear that conclusion of their story better than any other—unless it were her death. Better a thousand times than her marriage with Narramore!

In the morning, fatigue gave voice to conscience. He had bidden her go, when, perchance, a word would have checked her. Should he write, or even go to her straightway and retract what he had said? His will prevailed, and he did nothing.

The night that followed plagued him with other misgivings. It seemed more probable now that she had threatened what she would never have the courage to perform. She meant it at the moment—it declared a truth; but an hour after she would listen to common-place morality or prudence. Narramore would write to her; she might, perhaps, see him again. She would cling to the baser hope.

Might but the morrow bring him a letter from London!

It brought nothing; and day after day disappointed him. More than a week passed: he was ill with suspense, but could take no step for setting his mind at rest. Then, as he sat one morning at his work in the architect's office, there arrived a telegram addressed to him——

I must see you as soon as possible. Be here before six.—Narramore.

# CHAPTER XXVI

"What the devil does this mean, Hilliard?"

If never before, the indolent man was now thoroughly aroused. He had an open letter in his hand. Hilliard, standing before him in a little office that smelt of ledgers and gum, and many other commercial things, knew that the letter must be from Eve, and savagely hoped that it was dated London.

"This is from Miss Madeley, and it's all about you. Why couldn't you speak the other day?"

"What does she say about me?"

"That she has known you for a long time; that you saw a great deal of each other in London; that she has led you on with a hope of marrying her, though she never really meant it; in short, that she has used you very ill, and feels obliged now to make a clean breast of it."

The listener fixed his eye upon a copying-press, but without seeing it. A grim smile began to contort his lips.

"Where does she write from?"

"From her ordinary address—why not? I think this is rather too bad of you. Why didn't you speak, instead of writhing about and sputtering? That kind of thing is all very well—sense of honour and all that—but it meant that I was being taken in. Between friends—hang it! Of course I have done with her. I shall write at once. It's amazing;

it took away my breath. No doubt, though she doesn't say it, it was from you that she came to know of me. She began with a lie. And who the devil could have thought it! Her face—her way of talking! This will cut me up awfully. Of course, I'm sorry for you, too, but it was your plain duty to let me know what sort of a woman I had got hold of. Nay, it's she that has got hold of me, confound her! I don't feel myself! I'm thoroughly knocked over!''

Hilliard began humming an air. He crossed the room and sat down.

"Have you seen her since that Saturday?"

"No; she has made excuses, and I guessed something was wrong. What has been going on? *You* have seen her?"

"Of course."

Narramore glared.

"It's devilish underhand behaviour! Look here, old fellow, we're not going to quarrel. No woman is worth a quarrel between two old friends. But just speak out—can't you? What did you mean by keeping it from me?"

"It meant that I had nothing to say," Hilliard replied, through his moustache.

"You kept silence out of spite, then? You said to yourself, 'Let him marry her and find out afterwards what she really is!'"

"Nothing of the kind." He looked up frankly. "I saw no reason for speaking. She accuses herself without a shadow of reason; it's mere hysterical conscientiousness. We have known each other for half a year or so, and I have made love to her, but I never had the least encouragement. I knew all along she didn't care for me. How is she to blame? A girl is under no obligation to speak of all the men who have wanted to marry her, provided she has done nothing to be ashamed of. There's just one bit of insincerity. It's true she knew of you from me. But she looked you up because she despaired of finding employment; she was at an end of her money, didn't know what to do. I have heard this since I saw you last. It wasn't quite straightforward, but one can forgive it in a girl hard driven by necessity."

Narramore was listening with eagerness, his lips parted, and a growing hope in his eyes.

"There never was anything serious between you?"

"On her side, never for a moment. I pursued and pestered her, that was all."

"Do you mind telling me who the girl was that I saw you with at Dudley?"

"A friend of Miss Madeley's, over here from London on a holiday. I have tried to make use of her—to get her influence on my side——"

Narramore sprang from the corner of the table on which he had been sitting.

"Why couldn't she hold her tongue! That's just like a woman, to keep a thing quiet when she ought to speak of it, and bring it out when she had far better say nothing. I feel as if I had treated you badly, Hilliard. And the way you take it—I'd rather you eased your mind by swearing at me."

"I could swear hard enough. I could grip you by the throat and jump on you——"

"No, I'm hanged if you could!" He forced a laugh. "And I shouldn't advise you to try. Here, give me your hand instead." He seized it. "We're going to talk this over like two reasonable beings. Does this girl know her own mind? It seems to me from this letter that she wants to get rid of me."

"You must find out whether she does or not."

"Do you *think* she does?"

"I refuse to think about it at all."

"You mean she isn't worth troubling about? Tell the truth, and be hanged to you! Is she the kind of a girl a man may marry?"

"For all I know."

"Do you suspect her?" Narramore urged fiercely.

"She'll marry a rich man rather than a poor one—that's the worst I think of her."

"What woman won't?"

When question and answer had revolved about this point for another quarter of an hour, Hilliard brought the dialogue to an end. He was clay-colour, and perspiration stood on his forehead.

"You must make her out without any more help from me. I tell you the letter is all nonsense, and I can say no more."

He moved towards the exit.

"One thing I must know, Hilliard—Are you going to see her again?"

"Never—if I can help it."

"Can we be friends still?"

"If you never mention her name to me."

Again they shook hands, eyes crossing in a smile of shamed hostility. And the parting was for more than a twelvemonth.

Late in August, when Hilliard was thinking of a week's rest in the country, after a spell of harder and more successful work than he had ever previously known, he received a letter from Patty Ringrose.

"Dear Mr. Hilliard," wrote the girl, "I have just heard from Eve that she is to be married to Mr. Narramore in a week's time. She says you don't know about it; but I think you *ought* to know. I haven't been able to make anything of her two last letters, but she has written plainly at last. Perhaps she means me to tell you. Will you let me have a line? I should like to know whether you care much, and I do so hope you don't! I felt sure it would come to this, and if you'll believe me, it's just as well. I haven't answered her letter, and I don't know whether I shall. I might say disagreeable things. Everything is the same with me and always will be, I suppose." In conclusion, she was his sincerely. A postscript remarked: "They tell me I play better. I've been practising a great deal, just to kill the time."

"Dear Miss Ringrose," he responded, "I am very glad to know that Eve is to be comfortably settled for life. By all means answer her letter, and by all means keep from saying disagreeable things. It is never wise to quarrel with prosperous friends, and why should you? With every good wish——" he remained sincerely hers.

# CHAPTER XXVII

When Hilliard and his friend again shook hands it was the autumn of another year. Not even by chance had they encountered in the interval and no written message had passed between them. Their meeting was at a house newly acquired by the younger of the Birching brothers, who, being about to marry, summoned his bachelor familiars to smoke their pipes in the suburban abode while yet his rule there was undisputed. With Narramore he had of late resumed the friendship interrupted by Miss Birching's displeasure, for that somewhat imperious young lady, now the wife of an elderly ironmaster, moved in other circles; and Hilliard's professional value, which was beginning to be recognised by the Birchings otherwise than in the way of compliment, had overcome the restraints at first imposed by his dubious social standing.

They met genially, without a hint of estrangement.

"Your wife well?" Hilliard took an opportunity of asking apart.

"Thanks, she's getting all right again. At Llandudno just now. Glad to see that you're looking so uncommonly fit."

Hilliard had undoubtedly improved in personal appearance. He grew a beard, which added to his seeming age, but suited with his features; his carriage was more upright than of old.

A week or two after this, Narramore sent a friendly note——

"Shall I see you at Birching's on Sunday? My wife will be there, to meet Miss Marks and some other people. Come if you can, old fellow. I should take it as a great kindness."

And Hilliard went. In the hall he was confronted by Narramore, who shook hands with him rather effusively, and said a few words in an undertone.

"She's out in the garden. Will be delighted to see you. Awfully good of you, old boy! Had to come sooner or later, you know."

Not quite assured of this necessity, and something less than composed, Hilliard presently passed through the house into the large walled garden behind it. Here he was confusedly aware of a group of ladies, not one of whom, on drawing nearer, did he recognise. A succession of formalities discharged, he heard his friend's voice saying——

"Hilliard, let me introduce you to my wife."

There before him stood Eve. He had only just persuaded himself of her identity; his eyes searched her countenance with wonder which barely allowed him to assume a becoming attitude. But Mrs. Narramore was perfect in society's drill. She smiled very sweetly, gave her hand, said what the occasion demanded. Among the women present— all well bred—she suffered no obscurement. Her voice was tuned to the appropriate harmony; her talk invited to an avoidance of the hackneyed.

Hilliard revived his memories of Gower Place—of the streets of Paris. Nothing preternatural had come about; nothing that he had not forecasted in his hours of hope. But there were incidents in the past which this moment blurred away into the region of dreamland, and which he shrank from the effort of reinvesting with credibility.

"This is a pleasant garden."

Eve had approached him as he stood musing, after a conversation with other ladies.

"Rather new, of course; but a year will do wonders. Have you seen the chrysanthemums?"

She led him apart, as they stood regarding the flowers, Hilliard was surprised by words that fell from her.

"Your contempt for me is beyond expression, isn't it?"

"It is the last feeling I should associate with you," he answered.

"Oh, but be sincere. We have both learnt to speak another language—you no less than I. Let me hear a word such as you used to speak. I know you despise me unutterably."

"You are quite mistaken. I admire you very much."

"What—my skill? Or my dress?"

"Everything. You have become precisely what you were meant to be."

"Oh, the scorn of that!"

"I beg you not to think it for a moment. There was a time when I might have found a foolish pleasure in speaking to you with sarcasm. But that has long gone by."

"What am I, then?"

"An English lady—with rather more intellect than most."

Eve flushed with satisfaction.

"It's more than kind of you to say that. But you always had a generous spirit. I never thanked you. Not one poor word. I was cowardly—afraid to write. And you didn't care for my thanks."

"I do now."

"Then I thank you. With all my heart, again and again!"

Her voice trembled under fulness of meaning.

"You find life pleasant?"

"You do, I hope?" she answered, as they paced on.

"Not unpleasant, at all events. I am no longer slaving under the iron gods. I like my work, and it promises to reward me."

Eve made a remark about a flower-bed. Then her voice subdued again:

"How do you look back on your great venture—your attempt to make the most that could be made of a year in your life?"

"Quite contentedly. It was worth doing, and is worth remembering."

"Remember, if you care to," Eve resumed, "that all I am and have I owe to you. I was all but lost—all but a miserable captive for the rest of my life. You came and ransomed me. A less generous man would have spoilt his work at the last moment. But you were large-minded enough to support my weakness till I was safe."

Hilliard smiled for answer.

"You and Robert are friends again?"

"Perfectly."

She turned, and they rejoined the company.

A week later Hilliard went down into the country, to a quiet spot where he now and then refreshed his mind after toil in Birmingham. He slept at a cottage, and on the Sunday morning walked idly about the lanes.

A white frost had suddenly hastened the slow decay of mellow autumn. Low on the landscape lay a soft mist, dense enough to conceal everything at twenty yards away, but suffused with golden sunlight; overhead shone the clear blue sky. Roadside trees and hedges, their rich tints softened by the medium through which they were discerned, threw shadows of exquisite faintness. A perfect quiet possessed the air, but from every branch, as though shaken by some invisible hand, dead foliage dropped to earth in a continuous shower; softly pattering from beech to maple, or with the heavier fall of ash-leaves, while at long intervals sounded the thud of apples tumbling from a crab-tree. Thick-clustered berries arrayed the hawthorns, the briar was rich in scarlet fruit; everywhere the frost had left the adornment of its subtle artistry. Each leaf upon the hedge shone silver-out-lined; spiders' webs, woven from stem to stem, glistened in the morning radiance; the grasses by the wayside stood stark in gleaming mail.

And Maurice Hilliard, a free man in his own conceit, sang to himself a song of the joy of life.

# A CATALOGUE OF
# SELECTED DOVER BOOKS
# IN ALL FIELDS OF INTEREST

# A CATALOGUE OF SELECTED DOVER
# BOOKS IN ALL FIELDS OF INTEREST

CELESTIAL OBJECTS FOR COMMON TELESCOPES, T. W. Webb. The most used book in amateur astronomy: inestimable aid for locating and identifying nearly 4,000 celestial objects. Edited, updated by Margaret W. Mayall. 77 illustrations. Total of 645pp. 5⅜ x 8½.
20917-2, 20918-0 Pa., Two-vol. set $9.00

HISTORICAL STUDIES IN THE LANGUAGE OF CHEMISTRY, M. P. Crosland. The important part language has played in the development of chemistry from the symbolism of alchemy to the adoption of systematic nomenclature in 1892. ". . . wholeheartedly recommended,"—Science. 15 illustrations. 416pp. of text. 5⅝ x 8¼.
63702-6 Pa. $6.00

BURNHAM'S CELESTIAL HANDBOOK, Robert Burnham, Jr. Thorough, readable guide to the stars beyond our solar system. Exhaustive treatment, fully illustrated. Breakdown is alphabetical by constellation: Andromeda to Cetus in Vol. 1; Chamaeleon to Orion in Vol. 2; and Pavo to Vulpecula in Vol. 3. Hundreds of illustrations. Total of about 2000pp. 6⅛ x 9¼.
23567-X, 23568-8, 23673-0 Pa., Three-vol. set $26.85

THEORY OF WING SECTIONS: INCLUDING A SUMMARY OF AIR-FOIL DATA, Ira H. Abbott and A. E. von Doenhoff. Concise compilation of subatomic aerodynamic characteristics of modern NASA wing sections, plus description of theory. 350pp. of tables. 693pp. 5⅜ x 8½.
60586-8 Pa. $7.00

DE RE METALLICA, Georgius Agricola. Translated by Herbert C. Hoover and Lou H. Hoover. The famous Hoover translation of greatest treatise on technological chemistry, engineering, geology, mining of early modern times (1556). All 289 original woodcuts. 638pp. 6¾ x 11.
60006-8 Clothbd. $17.50

THE ORIGIN OF CONTINENTS AND OCEANS, Alfred Wegener. One of the most influential, most controversial books in science, the classic statement for continental drift. Full 1966 translation of Wegener's final (1929) version. 64 illustrations. 246pp. 5⅜ x 8½.
61708-4 Pa. $3.00

THE PRINCIPLES OF PSYCHOLOGY, William James. Famous long course complete, unabridged. Stream of thought, time perception, memory, experimental methods; great work decades ahead of its time. Still valid, useful; read in many classes. 94 figures. Total of 1391pp. 5⅜ x 8½.
20381-6, 20382-4 Pa., Two-vol. set $13.00

YUCATAN BEFORE AND AFTER THE CONQUEST, Diego de Landa. First English translation of basic book in Maya studies, the only significant account of Yucatan written in the early post-Conquest era. Translated by distinguished Maya scholar William Gates. Appendices, introduction, 4 maps and over 120 illustrations added by translator. 162pp. 5⅜ x 8½.
23622-6 Pa. $3.00

THE MALAY ARCHIPELAGO, Alfred R. Wallace. Spirited travel account by one of founders of modern biology. Touches on zoology, botany, ethnography, geography, and geology. 62 illustrations, maps. 515pp. 5⅜ x 8½.
20187-2 Pa. $6.95

THE DISCOVERY OF THE TOMB OF TUTANKHAMEN, Howard Carter, A. C. Mace. Accompany Carter in the thrill of discovery, as ruined passage suddenly reveals unique, untouched, fabulously rich tomb. Fascinating account, with 106 illustrations. New introduction by J. M. White. Total of 382pp. 5⅜ x 8½. (Available in U.S. only)     23500-9 Pa. $4.00

THE WORLD'S GREATEST SPEECHES, edited by Lewis Copeland and Lawrence W. Lamm. Vast collection of 278 speeches from Greeks up to present. Powerful and effective models; unique look at history. Revised to 1970. Indices. 842pp. 5⅜ x 8½.     20468-5 Pa. $8.95

THE 100 GREATEST ADVERTISEMENTS, Julian Watkins. The priceless ingredient; His master's voice; 99 44/100% pure; over 100 others. How they were written, their impact, etc. Remarkable record. 130 illustrations. 233pp. 7⅞ x 10 3/5.     20540-1 Pa. $5.00

CRUICKSHANK PRINTS FOR HAND COLORING, George Cruickshank. 18 illustrations, one side of a page, on fine-quality paper suitable for watercolors. Caricatures of people in society (c. 1820) full of trenchant wit. Very large format. 32pp. 11 x 16.     23684-6 Pa. $5.00

THIRTY-TWO COLOR POSTCARDS OF TWENTIETH-CENTURY AMERICAN ART, Whitney Museum of American Art. Reproduced in full color in postcard form are 31 art works and one shot of the museum. Calder, Hopper, Rauschenberg, others. Detachable. 16pp. 8¼ x 11.
23629-3 Pa. $2.50

MUSIC OF THE SPHERES: THE MATERIAL UNIVERSE FROM ATOM TO QUASAR SIMPLY EXPLAINED, Guy Murchie. Planets, stars, geology, atoms, radiation, relativity, quantum theory, light, antimatter, similar topics. 319 figures. 664pp. 5⅜ x 8½.
21809-0, 21810-4 Pa., Two-vol. set $10.00

EINSTEIN'S THEORY OF RELATIVITY, Max Born. Finest semi-technical account; covers Einstein, Lorentz, Minkowski, and others, with much detail, much explanation of ideas and math not readily available elsewhere on this level. For student, non-specialist. 376pp. 5⅜ x 8½.
60769-0 Pa. $4.00

THE COMPLETE BOOK OF DOLL MAKING AND COLLECTING, Catherine Christopher. Instructions, patterns for dozens of dolls, from rag doll on up to elaborate, historically accurate figures. Mould faces, sew clothing, make doll houses, etc. Also collecting information. Many illustrations. 288pp. 6 x 9.                                22066-4 Pa. $4.00

THE DAGUERREOTYPE IN AMERICA, Beaumont Newhall. Wonderful portraits, 1850's townscapes, landscapes; full text plus 104 photographs. The basic book. Enlarged 1976 edition. 272pp. 8¼ x 11¼.
23322-7 Pa. $6.00

CRAFTSMAN HOMES, Gustav Stickley. 296 architectural drawings, floor plans, and photographs illustrate 40 different kinds of "Mission-style" homes from *The Craftsman* (1901-16), voice of American style of simplicity and organic harmony. Thorough coverage of Craftsman idea in text and picture, now collector's item. 224pp. 8⅛ x 11.       23791-5 Pa. $6.00

PEWTER-WORKING: INSTRUCTIONS AND PROJECTS, Burl N. Osborn. & Gordon O. Wilber. Introduction to pewter-working for amateur craftsman. History and characteristics of pewter; tools, materials, step-by-step instructions. Photos, line drawings, diagrams. Total of 160pp. 7⅞ x 10¾.                                   23786-9 Pa. $3.50

THE GREAT CHICAGO FIRE, edited by David Lowe. 10 dramatic, eye-witness accounts of the 1871 disaster, including one of the aftermath and rebuilding, plus 70 contemporary photographs and illustrations of the ruins—courthouse, Palmer House, Great Central Depot, etc. Introduction by David Lowe. 87pp. 8¼ x 11.                   23771-0 Pa. $4.00

SILHOUETTES: A PICTORIAL ARCHIVE OF VARIED ILLUSTRA-TIONS, edited by Carol Belanger Grafton. Over 600 silhouettes from the 18th to 20th centuries include profiles and full figures of men and women, children, birds and animals, groups and scenes, nature, ships, an alphabet. Dozens of uses for commercial artists and craftspeople. 144pp. 8⅜ x 11¼.
23781-8 Pa. $4.00

ANIMALS: 1,419 COPYRIGHT-FREE ILLUSTRATIONS OF MAM-MALS, BIRDS, FISH, INSECTS, ETC., edited by Jim Harter. Clear wood engravings present, in extremely lifelike poses, over 1,000 species of ani-mals. One of the most extensive copyright-free pictorial sourcebooks of its kind. Captions. Index. 284pp. 9 x 12.                  23766-4 Pa. $7.50

INDIAN DESIGNS FROM ANCIENT ECUADOR, Frederick W. Shaffer. 282 original designs by pre-Columbian Indians of Ecuador (500-1500 A.D.). Designs include people, mammals, birds, reptiles, fish, plants, heads, geo-metric designs. Use as is or alter for advertising, textiles, leathercraft, etc. Introduction. 95pp. 8¾ x 11¼.                            23764-8 Pa. $3.50

SZIGETI ON THE VIOLIN, Joseph Szigeti. Genial, loosely structured tour by premier violinist, featuring a pleasant mixture of reminiscenes, insights into great music and musicians, innumerable tips for practicing violinists. 385 musical passages. 256pp. 5⅝ x 8¼.       23763-X Pa. $3.50

TONE POEMS, SERIES II: TILL EULENSPIEGELS LUSTIGE STREICHE, ALSO SPRACH ZARATHUSTRA, AND EIN HELDEN-LEBEN, Richard Strauss. Three important orchestral works, including very popular *Till Eulenspiegel's Marry Pranks*, reproduced in full score from original editions. Study score. 315pp. 9⅜ x 12¼. (Available in U.S. only) 23755-9 Pa. $7.50

TONE POEMS, SERIES I: DON JUAN, TOD UND VERKLARUNG AND DON QUIXOTE, Richard Strauss. Three of the most often performed and recorded works in entire orchestral repertoire, reproduced in full score from original editions. Study score. 286pp. 9⅜ x 12¼. (Available in U.S. only) 23754-0 Pa. $7.50

11 LATE STRING QUARTETS, Franz Joseph Haydn. The form which Haydn defined and "brought to perfection." *(Grove's)*. 11 string quartets in complete score, his last and his best. The first in a projected series of the complete Haydn string quartets. Reliable modern Eulenberg edition, otherwise difficult to obtain. 320pp. 8⅜ x 11¼. (Available in U.S. only) 23753-2 Pa. $6.95

FOURTH, FIFTH AND SIXTH SYMPHONIES IN FULL SCORE, Peter Ilyitch Tchaikovsky. Complete orchestral scores of Symphony No. 4 in F Minor, Op. 36; Symphony No. 5 in E Minor, Op. 64; Symphony No. 6 in B Minor, "Pathetique," Op. 74. Bretikopf & Hartel eds. Study score. 480pp. 9⅜ x 12¼. 23861-X Pa. $10.95

THE MARRIAGE OF FIGARO: COMPLETE SCORE, Wolfgang A. Mozart. Finest comic opera ever written. Full score, not to be confused with piano renderings. Peters edition. Study score. 448pp. 9⅜ x 12¼. (Available in U.S. only) 23751-6 Pa. $11.95

"IMAGE" ON THE ART AND EVOLUTION OF THE FILM, edited by Marshall Deutelbaum. Pioneering book brings together for first time 38 groundbreaking articles on early silent films from *Image* and 263 illustrations newly shot from rare prints in the collection of the International Museum of Photography. A landmark work. Index. 256pp. 8¼ x 11. 23777-X Pa. $8.95

AROUND-THE-WORLD COOKY BOOK, Lois Lintner Sumption and Marguerite Lintner Ashbrook. 373 cooky and frosting recipes from 28 countries (America, Austria, China, Russia, Italy, etc.) include Viennese kisses, rice wafers, London strips, lady fingers, hony, sugar spice, maple cookies, etc. Clear instructions. All tested. 38 drawings. 182pp. 5⅜ x 8. 23802-4 Pa. $2.50

THE ART NOUVEAU STYLE, edited by Roberta Waddell. 579 rare photographs, not available elsewhere, of works in jewelry, metalwork, glass, ceramics, textiles, architecture and furniture by 175 artists—Mucha, Seguy, Lalique, Tiffany, Gaudin, Hohlwein, Saarinen, and many others. 288pp. 8⅜ x 11¼. 23515-7 Pa. $6.95

THE AMERICAN SENATOR, Anthony Trollope. Little known, long un-available Trollope novel on a grand scale. Here are humorous comment on American vs. English culture, and stunning portrayal of a heroine/villainess. Superb evocation of Victorian village life. 561pp. 5⅜ x 8½.

23801-6 Pa. $6.00

WAS IT MURDER? James Hilton. The author of *Lost Horizon* and *Good-bye, Mr. Chips* wrote one detective novel (under a pen-name) which was quickly forgotten and virtually lost, even at the height of Hilton's fame. This edition brings it back—a finely crafted public school puzzle resplendent with Hilton's stylish atmosphere. A thoroughly English thriller by the creator of Shangri-la. 252pp. 5⅜ x 8. (Available in U.S. only)

23774-5 Pa. $3.00

CENTRAL PARK: A PHOTOGRAPHIC GUIDE, Victor Laredo and Henry Hope Reed. 121 superb photographs show dramatic views of Central Park: Bethesda Fountain, Cleopatra's Needle, Sheep Meadow, the Blockhouse, plus people engaged in many park activities: ice skating, bike riding, etc. Captions by former Curator of Central Park, Henry Hope Reed, provide historical view, changes, etc. Also photos of N.Y. landmarks on park's periphery. 96pp. 8½ x 11.

23750-8 Pa. $4.50

NANTUCKET IN THE NINETEENTH CENTURY, Clay Lancaster. 180 rare photographs, stereographs, maps, drawings and floor plans recreate unique American island society. Authentic scenes of shipwreck, light-houses, streets, homes are arranged in geographic sequence to provide walking-tour guide to old Nantucket existing today. Introduction, captions. 160pp. 8⅞ x 11¾.

23747-8 Pa. $6.95

STONE AND MAN: A PHOTOGRAPHIC EXPLORATION, Andreas Feininger. 106 photographs by *Life* photographer Feininger portray man's deep passion for stone through the ages. Stonehenge-like megaliths, fortified towns, sculpted marble and crumbling tenements show textures, beauties, fascination. 128pp. 9¼ x 10¾.

23756-7 Pa. $5.95

CIRCLES, A MATHEMATICAL VIEW, D. Pedoe. Fundamental aspects of college geometry, non-Euclidean geometry, and other branches of mathematics: representing circle by point. Poincare model, isoperimetric property, etc. Stimulating recreational reading. 66 figures. 96pp. 5⅝ x 8¼.

63698-4 Pa. $2.75

THE DISCOVERY OF NEPTUNE, Morton Grosser. Dramatic scientific history of the investigations leading up to the actual discovery of the eighth planet of our solar system. Lucid, well-researched book by well-known historian of science. 172pp. 5⅜ x 8½.

23726-5 Pa. $3.00

THE DEVIL'S DICTIONARY. Ambrose Bierce. Barbed, bitter, brilliant witticisms in the form of a dictionary. Best, most ferocious satire America has produced. 145pp. 5⅜ x 8½.

20487-1 Pa. $1.75

HISTORY OF BACTERIOLOGY, William Bulloch. The only comprehensive history of bacteriology from the beginnings through the 19th century. Special emphasis is given to biography-Leeuwenhoek, etc. Brief accounts of 350 bacteriologists form a separate section. No clearer, fuller study, suitable to scientists and general readers, has yet been written. 52 illustrations. 448pp. 5⅝ x 8¼. 23761-3 Pa. $6.50

THE COMPLETE NONSENSE OF EDWARD LEAR, Edward Lear. All nonsense limericks, zany alphabets, Owl and Pussycat, songs, nonsense botany, etc., illustrated by Lear. Total of 321pp. 5⅜ x 8½. (Available in U.S. only) 20167-8 Pa. $3.00

INGENIOUS MATHEMATICAL PROBLEMS AND METHODS, Louis A. Graham. Sophisticated material from Graham *Dial*, applied and pure; stresses solution methods. Logic, number theory, networks, inversions, etc. 237pp. 5⅜ x 8½. 20545-2 Pa. $3.50

BEST MATHEMATICAL PUZZLES OF SAM LOYD, edited by Martin Gardner. Bizarre, original, whimsical puzzles by America's greatest puzzler. From fabulously rare *Cyclopedia,* including famous 14-15 puzzles, the Horse of a Different Color, 115 more. Elementary math. 150 illustrations. 167pp. 5⅜ x 8½. 20498-7 Pa. $2.50

THE BASIS OF COMBINATION IN CHESS, J. du Mont. Easy-to-follow, instructive book on elements of combination play, with chapters on each piece and every powerful combination team—two knights, bishop and knight, rook and bishop, etc. 250 diagrams. 218pp. 5⅜ x 8½. (Available in U.S. only) 23644-7 Pa. $3.50

MODERN CHESS STRATEGY, Ludek Pachman. The use of the queen, the active king, exchanges, pawn play, the center, weak squares, etc. Section on rook alone worth price of the book. Stress on the moderns. Often considered the most important book on strategy. 314pp. 5⅜ x 8½. 20290-9 Pa. $3.50

LASKER'S MANUAL OF CHESS, Dr. Emanuel Lasker. Great world champion offers very thorough coverage of all aspects of chess. Combinations, position play, openings, end game, aesthetics of chess, philosophy of struggle, much more. Filled with analyzed games. 390pp. 5⅜ x 8½. 20640-8 Pa. $4.00

500 MASTER GAMES OF CHESS, S. Tartakower, J. du Mont. Vast collection of great chess games from 1798-1938, with much material nowhere else readily available. Fully annotated, arranged by opening for easier study. 664pp. 5⅜ x 8½. 23208-5 Pa. $6.00

A GUIDE TO CHESS ENDINGS, Dr. Max Euwe, David Hooper. One of the finest modern works on chess endings. Thorough analysis of the most frequently encountered endings by former world champion. 331 examples, each with diagram. 248pp. 5⅜ x 8½. 23332-4 Pa. $3.50

SECOND PIATIGORSKY CUP, edited by Isaac Kashdan. One of the greatest tournament books ever produced in the English language. All 90 games of the 1966 tournament, annotated by players, most annotated by both players. Features Petrosian, Spassky, Fischer, Larsen, six others. 228pp. 5⅜ x 8½. 23572-6 Pa. $3.50

ENCYCLOPEDIA OF CARD TRICKS, revised and edited by Jean Hugard. How to perform over 600 card tricks, devised by the world's greatest magicians: impromptus, spelling tricks, key cards, using special packs, much, much more. Additional chapter on card technique. 66 illustrations. 402pp. 5⅜ x 8½. (Available in U.S. only) 21252-1 Pa. $3.95

MAGIC: STAGE ILLUSIONS, SPECIAL EFFECTS AND TRICK PHOTOGRAPHY, Albert A. Hopkins, Henry R. Evans. One of the great classics; fullest, most authorative explanation of vanishing lady, levitations, scores of other great stage effects. Also small magic, automata, stunts. 446 illustrations. 556pp. 5⅜ x 8½. 23344-8 Pa. $5.00

THE SECRETS OF HOUDINI, J. C. Cannell. Classic study of Houdini's incredible magic, exposing closely-kept professional secrets and revealing, in general terms, the whole art of stage magic. 67 illustrations. 279pp. 5⅜ x 8½. 22913-0 Pa. $3.00

HOFFMANN'S MODERN MAGIC, Professor Hoffmann. One of the best, and best-known, magicians' manuals of the past century. Hundreds of tricks from card tricks and simple sleight of hand to elaborate illusions involving construction of complicated machinery. 332 illustrations. 563pp. 5⅜ x 8½. 23623-4 Pa. $6.00

MADAME PRUNIER'S FISH COOKERY BOOK, Mme. S. B. Prunier. More than 1000 recipes from world famous Prunier's of Paris and London, specially adapted here for American kitchen. Grilled tournedos with anchovy butter, Lobster a la Bordelaise, Prunier's prized desserts, more. Glossary. 340pp. 5⅜ x 8½. (Available in U.S. only) 22679-4 Pa. $3.00

FRENCH COUNTRY COOKING FOR AMERICANS, Louis Diat. 500 easy-to-make, authentic provincial recipes compiled by former head chef at New York's Fitz-Carlton Hotel: onion soup, lamb stew, potato pie, more. 309pp. 5⅜ x 8½. 23665-X Pa. $3.95

SAUCES, FRENCH AND FAMOUS, Louis Diat. Complete book gives over 200 specific recipes: bechamel, Bordelaise, hollandaise, Cumberland, apricot, etc. Author was one of this century's finest chefs, originator of vichyssoise and many other dishes. Index. 156pp. 5⅜ x 8. 23663-3 Pa. $2.50

TOLL HOUSE TRIED AND TRUE RECIPES, Ruth Graves Wakefield. Authentic recipes from the famous Mass. restaurant: popovers, veal and ham loaf, Toll House baked beans, chocolate cake crumb pudding, much more. Many helpful hints. Nearly 700 recipes. Index. 376pp. 5⅜ x 8½. 23560-2 Pa. $4.00

"OSCAR" OF THE WALDORF'S COOKBOOK, Oscar Tschirky. Famous American chef reveals 3455 recipes that made Waldorf great; cream of French, German, American cooking, in all categories. Full instructions, easy home use. 1896 edition. 907pp. 6⅝ x 9⅜.    20790-0 Clothbd. $15.00

COOKING WITH BEER, Carole Fahy. Beer has as superb an effect on food as wine, and at fraction of cost. Over 250 recipes for appetizers, soups, main dishes, desserts, breads, etc. Index. 144pp. 5⅜ x 8½. (Available in U.S. only)                                         23661-7 Pa. $2.50

STEWS AND RAGOUTS, Kay Shaw Nelson. This international cookbook offers wide range of 108 recipes perfect for everyday, special occasions, meals-in-themselves, main dishes. Economical, nutritious, easy-to-prepare: goulash, Irish stew, boeuf bourguignon, etc. Index. 134pp. 5⅜ x 8½.
23662-5 Pa. $2.50

DELICIOUS MAIN COURSE DISHES, Marian Tracy. Main courses are the most important part of any meal. These 200 nutritious, economical recipes from around the world make every meal a delight. "I . . . have found it so useful in my own household,"—N.Y. Times. Index. 219pp. 5⅜ x 8½.                                             23664-1 Pa. $3.00

FIVE ACRES AND INDEPENDENCE, Maurice G. Kains. Great back-to-the-land classic explains basics of self-sufficient farming: economics, plants, crops, animals, orchards, soils, land selection, host of other necessary things. Do not confuse with skimpy faddist literature; Kains was one of America's greatest agriculturalists. 95 illustrations. 397pp. 5⅜ x 8½.
20974-1 Pa. $3.95

A PRACTICAL GUIDE FOR THE BEGINNING FARMER, Herbert Jacobs. Basic, extremely useful first book for anyone thinking about moving to the country and starting a farm. Simpler than Kains, with greater emphasis on country living in general. 246pp. 5⅜ x 8½.
23675-7 Pa. $3.50

A GARDEN OF PLEASANT FLOWERS (PARADISI IN SOLE: PARADISUS TERRESTRIS), John Parkinson. Complete, unabridged reprint of first (1629) edition of earliest great English book on gardens and gardening. More than 1000 plants & flowers of Elizabethan, Jacobean garden fully described, most with woodcut illustrations. Botanically very reliable, a "speaking garden" of exceeding charm. 812 illustrations. 628pp. 8½ x 12¼.                                      23392-8 Clothbd. $25.00

ACKERMANN'S COSTUME PLATES, Rudolph Ackermann. Selection of 96 plates from the Repository of Arts, best published source of costume for English fashion during the early 19th century. 12 plates also in color. Captions, glossary and introduction by editor Stella Blum. Total of 120pp. 8⅜ x 11¼.                                           23690-0 Pa. $4.50

MUSHROOMS, EDIBLE AND OTHERWISE, Miron E. Hard. Profusely illustrated, very useful guide to over 500 species of mushrooms growing in the Midwest and East. Nomenclature updated to 1976. 505 illustrations. 628pp. 6½ x 9¼. 23309-X Pa. $7.95

AN ILLUSTRATED FLORA OF THE NORTHERN UNITED STATES AND CANADA, Nathaniel L. Britton, Addison Brown. Encyclopedic work covers 4666 species, ferns on up. Everything. Full botanical information, illustration for each. This earlier edition is preferred by many to more recent revisions. 1913 edition. Over 4000 illustrations, total of 2087pp. 6⅛ x 9¼. 22642-5, 22643-3, 22644-1 Pa., Three-vol. set $24.00

MANUAL OF THE GRASSES OF THE UNITED STATES, A. S. Hitchcock, U.S. Dept. of Agriculture. The basic study of American grasses, both indigenous and escapes, cultivated and wild. Over 1400 species. Full descriptions, information. Over 1100 maps, illustrations. Total of 1051pp. 5⅜ x 8½. 22717-0, 22718-9 Pa., Two-vol. set $12.00

THE CACTACEAE,, Nathaniel L. Britton, John N. Rose. Exhaustive, definitive. Every cactus in the world. Full botanical descriptions. Thorough statement of nomenclatures, habitat, detailed finding keys. The one book needed by every cactus enthusiast. Over 1275 illustrations. Total of 1080pp. 8 x 10¼. 21191-6, 21192-4 Clothbd., Two-vol. set $35.00

AMERICAN MEDICINAL PLANTS, Charles F. Millspaugh. Full descriptions, 180 plants covered: history; physical description; methods of preparation with all chemical constituents extracted; all claimed curative or adverse effects. 180 full-page plates. Classification table. 804pp. 6½ x 9¼. 23034-1 Pa. $10.00

A MODERN HERBAL, Margaret Grieve. Much the fullest, most exact, most useful compilation of herbal material. Gigantic alphabetical encyclopedia, from aconite to zedoary, gives botanical information, medical properties, folklore, economic uses, and much else. Indispensable to serious reader. 161 illustrations. 888pp. 6½ x 9¼. (Available in U.S. only) 22798-7, 22799-5 Pa., Two-vol. set $11.00

THE HERBAL or GENERAL HISTORY OF PLANTS, John Gerard. The 1633 edition revised and enlarged by Thomas Johnson. Containing almost 2850 plant descriptions and 2705 superb illustrations, Gerard's *Herbal* is a monumental work, the book all modern English herbals are derived from, the one herbal every serious enthusiast should have in its entirety. Original editions are worth perhaps $750. 1678pp. 8½ x 12¼. 23147-X Clothbd. $50.00

MANUAL OF THE TREES OF NORTH AMERICA, Charles S. Sargent. The basic survey of every native tree and tree-like shrub, 717 species in all. Extremely full descriptions, information on habitat, growth, locales, economics, etc. Necessary to every serious tree lover. Over 100 finding keys. 783 illustrations. Total of 986pp. 5⅜ x 8½. 20277-1, 20278-X Pa., Two-vol. set $10.00

AMERICAN BIRD ENGRAVINGS, Alexander Wilson et al. All 76 plates. from Wilson's *American Ornithology* (1808-14), most important ornithological work before Audubon, plus 27 plates from the supplement (1825-33) by Charles Bonaparte. Over 250 birds portrayed. 8 plates also reproduced in full color. 111pp. 9⅜ x 12½. 23195-X Pa. $6.00

CRUICKSHANK'S PHOTOGRAPHS OF BIRDS OF AMERICA, Allan D. Cruickshank. Great ornithologist, photographer presents 177 closeups, groupings, panoramas, flightings, etc., of about 150 different birds. Expanded *Wings in the Wilderness*. Introduction by Helen G. Cruickshank. 191pp. 8¼ x 11. 23497-5 Pa. $6.00

AMERICAN WILDLIFE AND PLANTS, A. C. Martin, et al. Describes food habits of more than 1000 species of mammals, birds, fish. Special treatment of important food plants. Over 300 illustrations. 500pp. 5⅜ x 8½. 20793-5 Pa. $4.95

THE PEOPLE CALLED SHAKERS, Edward D. Andrews. Lifetime of research, definitive study of Shakers: origins, beliefs, practices, dances, social organization, furniture and crafts, impact on 19th-century USA, present heritage. Indispensable to student of American history, collector. 33 illustrations. 351pp. 5⅜ x 8½. 21081-2 Pa. $4.00

OLD NEW YORK IN EARLY PHOTOGRAPHS, Mary Black. New York City as it was in 1853-1901, through 196 wonderful photographs from N.-Y. Historical Society. Great Blizzard, Lincoln's funeral procession, great buildings. 228pp. 9 x 12. 22907-6 Pa. $7.95

MR. LINCOLN'S CAMERA MAN: MATHEW BRADY, Roy Meredith. Over 300 Brady photos reproduced directly from original negatives, photos. Jackson, Webster, Grant, Lee, Carnegie, Barnum; Lincoln; Battle Smoke, Death of Rebel Sniper, Atlanta Just After Capture. Lively commentary. 368pp. 8⅜ x 11¼. 23021-X Pa. $8.95

TRAVELS OF WILLIAM BARTRAM, William Bartram. From 1773-8, Bartram explored Northern Florida, Georgia, Carolinas, and reported on wild life, plants, Indians, early settlers. Basic account for period, entertaining reading. Edited by Mark Van Doren. 13 illustrations. 141pp. 5⅜ x 8½. 20013-2 Pa. $4.50

THE GENTLEMAN AND CABINET MAKER'S DIRECTOR, Thomas Chippendale. Full reprint, 1762 style book, most influential of all time; chairs, tables, sofas, mirrors, cabinets, etc. 200 plates, plus 24 photographs of surviving pieces. 249pp. 9⅞ x 12¾. 21601-2 Pa. $6.50

AMERICAN CARRIAGES, SLEIGHS, SULKIES AND CARTS, edited by Don H. Berkebile. 168 Victorian illustrations from catalogues, trade journals, fully captioned. Useful for artists. Author is Assoc. Curator, Div. of Transportation of Smithsonian Institution. 168pp. 8½ x 9½. 23328-6 Pa. $5.00

THE SENSE OF BEAUTY, George Santayana. Masterfully written discussion of nature of beauty, materials of beauty, form, expression; art, literature, social sciences all involved. 168pp. 5⅜ x 8½.        20238-0 Pa. $2.50

ON THE IMPROVEMENT OF THE UNDERSTANDING, Benedict Spinoza. Also contains *Ethics, Correspondence,* all in excellent R. Elwes translation. Basic works on entry to philosophy, pantheism, exchange of ideas with great contemporaries. 402pp. 5⅜ x 8½.        20250-X Pa. $4.50

THE TRAGIC SENSE OF LIFE, Miguel de Unamuno. Acknowledged masterpiece of existential literature, one of most important books of 20th century. Introduction by Madariaga. 367pp. 5⅜ x 8½.
                                                        20257-7 Pa. $3.50

THE GUIDE FOR THE PERPLEXED, Moses Maimonides. Great classic of medieval Judaism attempts to reconcile revealed religion (Pentateuch, commentaries) with Aristotelian philosophy. Important historically, still relevant in problems. Unabridged Friedlander translation. Total of 473pp. 5⅜ x 8½.                                        20351-4 Pa. $5.00

THE I CHING (THE BOOK OF CHANGES), translated by James Legge. Complete translation of basic text plus appendices by Confucius, and Chinese commentary of most penetrating divination manual ever prepared. Indispensable to study of early Oriental civilizations, to modern inquiring reader. 448pp. 5⅜ x 8½.                                21062-6 Pa. $4.00

THE EGYPTIAN BOOK OF THE DEAD, E. A. Wallis Budge. Complete reproduction of Ani's papyrus, finest ever found. Full hieroglyphic text, interlinear transliteration, word for word translation, smooth translation. Basic work, for Egyptology, for modern study of psychic matters. Total of 533pp. 6½ x 9¼. (Available in U.S. only)                21866-X Pa. $4.95

THE GODS OF THE EGYPTIANS, E. A. Wallis Budge. Never excelled for richness, fullness: all gods, goddesses, demons, mythical figures of Ancient Egypt; their legends, rites, incarnations, variations, powers, etc. Many hieroglyphic texts cited. Over 225 illustrations, plus 6 color plates. Total of 988pp. 6⅛ x 9¼. (Available in U.S. only)
                                22055-9, 22056-7 Pa., Two-vol. set $12.00

THE ENGLISH AND SCOTTISH POPULAR BALLADS, Francis J. Child. Monumental, still unsuperseded; all known variants of Child ballads, commentary on origins, literary references, Continental parallels, other features. Added: papers by G. L. Kittredge, W. M. Hart. Total of 2761pp. 6½ x 9¼.
    21409-5, 21410-9, 21411-7, 21412-5, 21413-3 Pa., Five-vol. set $37.50

CORAL GARDENS AND THEIR MAGIC, Bronsilaw Malinowski. Classic study of the methods of tilling the soil and of agricultural rites in the Trobriand Islands of Melanesia. Author is one of the most important figures in the field of modern social anthropology. 143 illustrations. Indexes. Total of 911pp. of text. 5⅝ x 8¼. (Available in U.S. only)
                                                        23597-1 Pa. $12.95

THE PHILOSOPHY OF HISTORY, Georg W. Hegel. Great classic of Western thought develops concept that history is not chance but a rational process, the evolution of freedom. 457pp. 5⅜ x 8½.    20112-0 Pa. $4.50

LANGUAGE, TRUTH AND LOGIC, Alfred J. Ayer. Famous, clear introduction to Vienna, Cambridge schools of Logical Positivism. Role of philosophy, elimination of metaphysics, nature of analysis, etc. 160pp. 5⅜ x 8½. (Available in U.S. only)    20010-8 Pa. $1.75

A PREFACE TO LOGIC, Morris R. Cohen. Great City College teacher in renowned, easily followed exposition of formal logic, probability, values, logic and world order and similar topics; no previous background needed. 209pp. 5⅜ x 8½.    23517-3 Pa. $3.50

REASON AND NATURE, Morris R. Cohen. Brilliant analysis of reason and its multitudinous ramifications by charismatic teacher. Interdisciplinary, synthesizing work widely praised when it first appeared in 1931. Second (1953) edition. Indexes. 496pp. 5⅜ x 8½.    23633-1 Pa. $6.00

AN ESSAY CONCERNING HUMAN UNDERSTANDING, John Locke. The only complete edition of enormously important classic, with authoritative editorial material by A. C. Fraser. Total of 1176pp. 5⅜ x 8½.
20530-4, 20531-2 Pa., Two-vol. set $14.00

HANDBOOK OF MATHEMATICAL FUNCTIONS WITH FORMULAS, GRAPHS, AND MATHEMATICAL TABLES, edited by Milton Abramowitz and Irene A. Stegun. Vast compendium: 29 sets of tables, some to as high as 20 places. 1,046pp. 8 x 10½.    61272-4 Pa. $14.95

MATHEMATICS FOR THE PHYSICAL SCIENCES, Herbert S. Wilf. Highly acclaimed work offers clear presentations of vector spaces and matrices, orthogonal functions, roots of polynomial equations, conformal mapping, calculus of variations, etc. Knowledge of theory of functions of real and complex variables is assumed. Exercises and solutions. Index. 284pp. 5⅝ x 8¼.    63635-6 Pa. $4.50

THE PRINCIPLE OF RELATIVITY, Albert Einstein et al. Eleven most important original papers on special and general theories. Seven by Einstein, two by Lorentz, one each by Minkowski and Weyl. All translated, unabridged. 216pp. 5⅜ x 8½.    60081-5 Pa. $3.00

THERMODYNAMICS, Enrico Fermi. A classic of modern science. Clear, organized treatment of systems, first and second laws, entropy, thermodynamic potentials, gaseous reactions, dilute solutions, entropy constant. No math beyond calculus required. Problems. 160pp. 5⅜ x 8½.
60361-X Pa. $2.75

ELEMENTARY MECHANICS OF FLUIDS, Hunter Rouse. Classic undergraduate text widely considered to be far better than many later books. Ranges from fluid velocity and acceleration to role of compressibility in fluid motion. Numerous examples, questions, problems. 224 illustrations. 376pp. 5⅝ x 8¼.    63699-2 Pa. $5.00

AN AUTOBIOGRAPHY, Margaret Sanger. Exciting personal account of hard-fought battle for woman's right to birth control, against prejudice, church, law. Foremost feminist document. 504pp. 5⅜ x 8½.
20470-7 Pa. $5.50

MY BONDAGE AND MY FREEDOM, Frederick Douglass. Born as a slave, Douglass became outspoken force in antislavery movement. The best of Douglass's autobiographies. Graphic description of slave life. Introduction by P. Foner. 464pp. 5⅜ x 8½.
22457-0 Pa. $5.00

LIVING MY LIFE, Emma Goldman. Candid, no holds barred account by foremost American anarchist: her own life, anarchist movement, famous contemporaries, ideas and their impact. Struggles and confrontations in America, plus deportation to U.S.S.R. Shocking inside account of persecution of anarchists under Lenin. 13 plates. Total of 944pp. 5⅜ x 8½.
22543-7, 22544-5 Pa., Two-vol. set $9.00

LETTERS AND NOTES ON THE MANNERS, CUSTOMS AND CONDITIONS OF THE NORTH AMERICAN INDIANS, George Catlin. Classic account of life among Plains Indians: ceremonies, hunt, warfare, etc. Dover edition reproduces for first time all original paintings. 312 plates. 572pp. of text. 6⅛ x 9¼.
22118-0, 22119-9 Pa.. Two-vol. set $10.00

THE MAYA AND THEIR NEIGHBORS, edited by Clarence L. Hay, others. Synoptic view of Maya civilization in broadest sense, together with Northern, Southern neighbors. Integrates much background, valuable detail not elsewhere. Prepared by greatest scholars: Kroeber, Morley, Thompson, Spinden, Vaillant, many others. Sometimes called Tozzer Memorial Volume. 60 illustrations, linguistic map. 634pp. 5⅜ x 8½.
23510-6 Pa. $7.50

HANDBOOK OF THE INDIANS OF CALIFORNIA, A. L. Kroeber. Foremost American anthropologist offers complete ethnographic study of each group. Monumental classic. 459 illustrations, maps. 995pp. 5⅜ x 8½.
23368-5 Pa. $10.00

SHAKTI AND SHAKTA, Arthur Avalon. First book to give clear, cohesive analysis of Shakta doctrine, Shakta ritual and Kundalini Shakti (yoga). Important work by one of world's foremost students of Shaktic and Tantric thought. 732pp. 5⅜ x 8½. (Available in U.S. only)
23645-5 Pa. $7.95

AN INTRODUCTION TO THE STUDY OF THE MAYA HIEROGLYPHS, Syvanus Griswold Morley. Classic study by one of the truly great figures in hieroglyph research. Still the best introduction for the student for reading Maya hieroglyphs. New introduction by J. Eric S. Thompson. 117 illustrations. 284pp. 5⅜ x 8½.
23108-9 Pa. $4.00

A STUDY OF MAYA ART, Herbert J. Spinden. Landmark classic interprets Maya symbolism, estimates styles, covers ceramics, architecture, murals, stone carvings as artforms. Still a basic book in area. New introduction by J. Eric Thompson. Over 750 illustrations. 341pp. 8⅜ x 11¼.
21235-1 Pa. $6.95

THE STANDARD BOOK OF QUILT MAKING AND COLLECTING, Marguerite Ickis. Full information, full-sized patterns for making 46 traditional quilts, also 150 other patterns. Quilted cloths, lame, satin quilts, etc. 483 illustrations. 273pp. 6⅞ x 9⅝.          20582-7 Pa. $4.50

ENCYCLOPEDIA OF VICTORIAN NEEDLEWORK, S. Caulfield, Blanche Saward. Simply inexhaustible gigantic alphabetical coverage of every traditional needlecraft—stitches, materials, methods, tools, types of work; definitions, many projects to be made. 1200 illustrations; double-columned text. 697pp. 8⅛ x 11.          22800-2, 22801-0 Pa., Two-vol. set $12.00

MECHANICK EXERCISES ON THE WHOLE ART OF PRINTING, Joseph Moxon. First complete book (1683-4) ever written about typography, a compendium of everything known about printing at the latter part of 17th century. Reprint of 2nd (1962) Oxford Univ. Press edition. 74 illustrations. Total of 550pp. 6⅛ x 9¼.          23617-X Pa. $7.95

PAPERMAKING, Dard Hunter. Definitive book on the subject by the foremost authority in the field. Chapters dealing with every aspect of history of craft in every part of the world. Over 320 illustrations. 2nd, revised and enlarged (1947) edition. 672pp. 5⅜ x 8½.          23619-6 Pa. $7.95

THE ART DECO STYLE, edited by Theodore Menten. Furniture, jewelry, metalwork, ceramics, fabrics, lighting fixtures, interior decors, exteriors, graphics from pure French sources. Best sampling around. Over 400 photographs. 183pp. 8⅜ x 11¼.          22824-X Pa. $5.00

*Prices subject to change without notice.*

Available at your book dealer or write for free catalogue to Dept. GI, Dover Publications, Inc., 180 Varick St., N.Y., N.Y. 10014. Dover publishes more than 175 books each year on science, elementary and advanced mathematics, biology, music, art, literary history, social sciences and other areas.